Becky Bigteeth

BECKY BIGTEETH

and the BATTLE of ELFARON

Dan Watford

Dan Watford

This is a work of fiction. Names, characters, organisations, places, events, and incidents are either products of the author's imagination or are used fictitiously. Any resemblance to actual persons, living or dead, or actual events is purely coincidental.

ISBN: 978-1-5272-5313-1

CHAPTER 1

Becky slipped over several times on her way up the hill. It didn't matter, her clothes were already covered in mud and the only part of her face that was clean was under her eyes where her tears had washed away the mud. Blood was still pouring out of her nose but that didn't matter either. All that mattered to Becky, was making it to the top of the hill and into the castle, her safe haven.

Eventually she made it to the top of the hill and into Peveril Castle. This was where she came when she got too upset to go home, where she came when the bullies had won. They had most certainly won today. Once she was inside the castle, she climbed up the stairs and perched herself on the ledge of her favourite window, the one that overlooked the magnificent Peak District.

Becky could sit here for hours, admiring the view, watching the miles and miles of fields, hills and mountains. She liked to watch the sheep in the fields grazing on the grass, blissfully ignorant of the pain and suffering going on in the world while they chomped away. She also liked to watch the birds fly high above her head, she envied their freedom and their ability to fly far away from any danger as soon as they spot it.

She looked over at Mam Tor, her family's favourite mountain, where they would often go rambling, stopping for picnics and admiring the view. She looked out and imagined she was a bird, and wished she could fly far away from here, far away from her tormentors, far away from her misery.

CHAPTER 2

Becky hadn't always been bullied, far from it. When she first started at Castleton Primary School, she made lots of friends, was always chatty and made sure to speak to everyone. Becky's best friend at primary school was Hatty Heckstrom.

The pair of them were inseparable. Hatty lived on the next street and would knock on Aunt Sylvia's door every morning to call on Becky. They would walk to school together, hand in hand, skipping and singing as they went. Once they got to class, they would sit next to each other all day and talk non-stop until the teachers shushed them.

Things changed for Becky when she was eight years old, when her teeth had started to grow to their abnormal size. Her baby teeth were a normal size before they fell out but her adult teeth were huge, they were perfectly straight and lovely and white but that didn't hide the fact that they were massive.

Becky also had two different colour eyes. Her left eye was emerald green while her right eye was ice blue. Her eyes were striking, but unfortunately, they weren't striking enough to distract from her teeth. They were a result of a condition called Heterochromia and they never caused Becky any problems, no-one ever bullied her about them. If anything they helped to make her special and stand out when she was young. But once her teeth had grown as well, this was too much for the other children to take and Becky started to hear them calling her names behind her back and avoiding her.

It was nothing serious at first and Becky was able to shrug it off with the support of Hatty who stood by her despite Becky being singled out by most of the other kids at school. 'She's weird' they'd say to each other, 'don't play with her or you'll get giant teeth as well.' Although Becky was upset by it, she was still able to carry on being her cheerful self, but that all changed after the summer holidays leading up to their last year at primary school.

Hatty would normally spend most of the holidays round Aunt Sylvia's house, playing with Becky or they'd be out in the Peak District walking and having picnics. But this year Hatty had gone to stay with her cousin on the south coast for the last four weeks of the holiday, meaning Becky didn't see her again until they started back at school.

Becky was surprised that Hatty hadn't knocked on her door on her way to school that morning but hadn't thought much of it. When she saw Hatty in the playground before class she ran up to her and went to give her a big hug, delighted to have her best friend back.

'Hatty! Hatty!' Becky screamed, running towards her but Hatty wasn't returning her smile, in fact she looked disgusted for some reason.

'Urgh, get away from me, you freak.' Hatty shouted as she pushed Becky away. 'Don't come near me with those massive teeth, you might bite my face off.' Becky stood open mouthed, she was in too much shock to react, a crowd was gathering, they were laughing along with Hatty. 'You belong in a zoo not in a school, Becky Bigteeth.'

Becky Bigteeth

The other kids all started laughing at Becky's new nickname. 'Becky Bigteeth, Becky Bigteeth.' They all started chanting together as more and more kids joined in. Becky looked round at the other kids, half of them had also been friends with her last year, but now they were all pointing and laughing at her.

She looked back at Hatty, hoping that she was joking and would start laughing and hug Becky so the others would stop, but Hatty just stood there with a look of disgust. The look on Hatty's face hurt Becky more than the words, the fact that Hatty actually looked disgusted by her. Becky dropped her gaze, started crying and ran out the school gates as fast as she could.

CHAPTER 3

That had been the first time Becky had run up to Peveril Castle to be on her own. It was the first of many as from that day on, Becky's life became more and more miserable. As the school year went on, she lost every friend she had. Hatty was always at the centre of the bullying, Becky spent so many nights lying awake in bed crying and wondering what could possibly have happened to Hatty that summer to make her be so cruel and unkind to her former best friend.

She'd tried speaking to Hatty when she was on her own but Hatty just screamed at her to leave her alone so she guessed she'd never know now. Some people just change, that's what her cousin Esme had told her when she'd come home from school to find Becky crying on the sofa. Becky guessed that was as good an answer as any, some people just change, Becky didn't wish she'd change but she sure wished her teeth would.

Becky lived with her cousin Esme and Esme's mother, Aunt Sylvia. Her aunt had adopted Becky and brought her to live in Castleton when Becky's mother had disowned her and abandoned her as a baby. They never spoke of Becky's mother, or her father, who had never been involved in her life. For a while, Becky had been very interested in her parents and asked Sylvia about them and where they were now, but Sylvia just started crying whenever she brought it up, so Becky had stopped asking long ago.

Becky Bigteeth

Esme is a couple of years older than Becky, she has fairly big teeth but nowhere near as big as Becky's and everyone agrees that Esme is beautiful. Her flowing dark hair compliment her dark eyes and if anything, her teeth just help Esme to stand out more. Esme is also the nicest person Becky knows, she always looks out for Becky and gets her involved in as many different activities as she can.

They go dancing together every Tuesday night at Delphine's Dance Studio and every Thursday night they go to karate classes, taught by Coach Colby in the village hall. They've been going to both these classes for about six months now. Esme dragged Becky along to karate one night when Becky had suffered a particularly horrible day at school and couldn't stop crying. Becky hadn't wanted to go, worrying that she'd just make a fool out of herself but Esme insisted.

To her surprise though, she actually really enjoyed it and Coach Colby had been really nice to her and made her laugh. He was very extravagant and flamboyant and moved with a smoothness Becky had never seen before. When he walked, it looked to Becky like he was gliding along the ground, his whole body in perfect harmony. He spoke with such enthusiasm and sincerity that Becky couldn't help but smile along and feel like they were genuinely friends. She always remembered the first thing he said to her once Esme had introduced them. He shook her hand and smiled at her with such warmth.

'My, my' he said, 'what a pleasure this is, you move like a true warrior, I can tell you're going to do very special things in my class.' Becky went red and looked over at Esme and started to giggle, that's when he noticed her teeth. 'And look at your teeth' he said, 'they're, they're' Becky waited for him to laugh or say something insulting, 'they're incredible!' he finished. Becky couldn't believe it, he actually seemed to think her teeth were nice, no-one had ever said her teeth were incredible before. She had beamed for the rest of the night, going gung-ho in the karate class without a care in the world and learning how to defend herself should she ever have to. Little did she know back then just how much self-defence she'd need.

CHAPTER 4

A s Becky sat in the window ledge, replaying what had happened at school today. She felt like she should have used her self-defence but things had just happened so suddenly, and she was so outnumbered there probably wasn't a great deal she could have done.

The school day had started pretty much how it usually did, Becky walked to school on her own, keeping her head down whenever she saw a group of other children so they didn't notice her and start calling her names.

Once she got to school, she went to the library to read, the library was pretty much a safe haven at school, the cool kids rarely went in there and if they did, they couldn't bully her much because Mrs Jackson, the librarian was always monitoring the noise and wouldn't stand for any unruly behaviour.

Becky would generally read in the library until the bell for first class would go, then she'd hurry along to class, this morning it was double science, and sit at the front. She'd still get called names by the other kids, but she found that the closer she got to a teacher the further away she got from the name calling.

Double science ticked along as double lessons usually do, the first half taking an age, the second half even longer, but eventually the bell rang for lunch and the kids ran out as fast as they could. All except Becky who had learned that it paid for her to wait until the queue in the dining hall had died down. She waited until the classroom was empty before bidding Mr Stephens, the science teacher, goodbye, then she made her way down the corridor to the rat run that was the dining hall.

Becky hated the looks she got from the dinner ladies, half pity, half fascination. They always seemed to want to ask her to show them her teeth, but they'd never come straight out and say it. She ordered her jacket potato with butter and cheese and took her tray to find an empty table.

There weren't any, but she did manage to find a seat near some of the nicer kids who, rather than bully her, would instead look at her with sympathy and tolerate her on their table. As long as she didn't talk to them though, the other kids would be bullied just for talking to her.

She ate her lunch and went out to get some fresh air, it had been raining all morning but had stopped just before lunchtime. It nearly always rained in the Peak District, her Aunt Sylvia always said it rained so much because God liked to water the beautiful landscape.

Becky was too busy staring at the ground to even see the football coming towards her. She had no idea what hit her when it came crashing into her face, hitting her nose first, it sent her sprawling to the ground in a heap. Hatty came running up, squealing with delight.

'Did you see that?' Hatty asked the others, who she'd been playing football with, 'did you see that?' she asked again still squealing. 'Right on her nose, bullseye! Fifty points to Hatty! Ssssttttrrrrrike!' Hatty roared with laughter again and bent double as her cronies all started clapping and cheering her. Becky was

Becky Bigteeth

lying in a puddle on the ground holding her nose, she had no idea what had just happened but she'd recognise that horrible laugh anywhere.

She was just getting to her feet, trying to regain her senses when someone shoved her from behind and she landed, head first, in the puddle again. Hatty and her friends were all stood around Becky, circling her, laughing and pointing. The boy who had pushed her over, Wayne Patterson, stood with his arms in the air, jubilant that he'd managed to push over someone half his size, who wasn't even looking.

'Get up, Freakshow' Hatty shouted at Becky, 'you'd better not have burst our football with your giant teeth. Now go and fetch it.' She shouted, pointing Becky into the direction of the football. Becky's eyes were watering so much she couldn't see anything and just stood in front of Hatty with one hand holding her nose, trying to stem the bleeding and the other hand wiping her eyes.

'What are you waiting for?' Hatty asked, 'I said, go and fetch the bloody ball.' Becky looked round, she could just about make out the ball in the direction Hatty was pointing but as she went to get it someone stuck their leg out and she went flying again. There were about thirty kids all in the crowd now, all laughing their heads off, Becky had landed face down in the mud and was just getting back up when she heard shouting.

'What's going on here?' Said Mr Stephens at the top of his voice.

'Nothing, Sir' said Hatty as she leant down and grabbed Becky by the arm to pull her up, pinching her arm as she did. 'Don't say a word.' Hatty whispered to Becky as she pulled her to her feet.

'Becky?' asked Mr Stephens, 'what's going on? Are you okay?'

11

'Yes, fine, Mr Stephens' said Becky, 'sorry, I wasn't looking where I was going and fell over, Hatty was just helping me up.'

'Yes, that's right, Sir' said Hatty, 'there you go, Becky, you silly billy, try to look where you're going next time.' Hatty pretended to help straighten Becky's jacket which was now covered in mud.

'Very well' said Mr Stephens, 'you'd better get yourself to the nurse to get your nose checked out, Becky. And after that get yourself home to get changed, come back this afternoon.'

'Yes, Mr Stephens, I will' said Becky and she shuffled off towards the nurse's office but as she turned the corner she ran. Out the school grounds she went and up towards Peveril Castle. Where she now sat, cold and shivering in the window, wishing she could fly far away from here, far away from her tormentors. She didn't know where she'd fly to, as long as it was somewhere where she wasn't picked on, she wished for so long and so hard that she fell asleep on the concrete floor.

CHAPTER 5

Wake up, Becky' said Esme, gently shaking her cousin awake. Becky shook her head and looked round, it was starting to get dark.

'What time is it?' she asked and winced, feeling the pain in her nose come straight back.

'Just gone six' said Esme, 'we've been worried, mum had a call from Mr Stephens at school, he told her you'd gone home to get changed and not gone back to school. I thought you'd be up here. Oh Becs, look at your face, you poor thing.' Esme wrapped her arms round her.

When they stopped hugging, Becky looked at the ground and nodded her head, it took her a few moments to compose herself, 'it's horrible, Esme' she said. 'They just won't stop. No matter what I do, talk to them, ignore them, keep my head down, try and stay away from them. It makes no difference, they find me eventually and when they do...' Becky stopped talking as her tears took over, Esme hugged her again.

'It's okay, Becs' Esme said, still hugging her, 'you'll see, it will all be alright.'

Becky broke the hug and moved back slightly, giving herself some room, 'no, it won't be Esme, you don't understand, they just won't leave me alone. I'm not going back, I can't, they won't stop until they've completely broken me, I won't give them the satisfaction. I'd sooner stay home and never go outside than have to keep facing them at school.'

Esme looked at Becky unsure what to do or say, she was normally really good at calming her cousin down. 'Come on then, let's go and talk to mum, you can get warm and we'll have some dinner.'

Esme put her arm round Becky as they made their way down the steps of the castle and down the hill towards their house on Narrow Street. 'I'm serious Esme, I know you think I'm overreacting but I'm really not. I'm not going back, I'll just go to school in Derby, I could catch the bus early in the morning, it would be fun, plus, I'd be less noticeable in a big city. I'm sure people in the city are too busy living their own lives to worry about someone with giant teeth like me. Or maybe we could move house, you know, all of us, we could move somewhere new and start afresh, too many people know me here, too many people hate me.' Becky felt herself on the verge of tears again so bit her lip and they walked the rest of the way in silence.

CHAPTER 6

They got to the house just before the rain started again. 'Hi mum' Esme shouted as they walked in, 'found her, there's nothing to worry about.' Becky and Esme took their coats off in the hallway, they lived at number 12 which is a three-bedroom mid terrace cottage right at the bottom of the hill that leads up to Peveril Castle.

The house was small, but homely, it was always warm because Aunt Sylvia liked to keep the fire in. It didn't matter how what the weather was like outside, Sylvia would have a fire in, she suffered from a crooked back which hurt her constantly, the only way she could combat the pain was to keep as warm as possible at all times. This meant keeping a fire in all year round and whenever she went out in moderately cold weather she would layer up to the point of being unrecognisable, rather than a woman walking down the street she looked like a walking jumble sale. Couple that with the cane she sometimes needed to help her walk and the kids in Castleton had a field day teasing her.

Just a trip to the shops would entail Sylvia spending fifteen minutes layering up and psyching herself up for the cold, only to get outside and have to ignore the children yelling Hunchback of Notre Dame at her or calling her a witch. She'd been called all sorts over the years but she never let it bother her. Becky admired her aunt for her resiliency but at the same time she couldn't help but think that if her aunt was a bit more normal Becky herself would probably get bullied less.

Sylvia was sat by the fire keeping warm when they came in, she struggled to get up so Esme told her to stay where she was, then she sent Becky upstairs to get showered and changed before dinner. 'A nice warm shower is what you need, Becs' she said, 'wash that depression off as well as the mud and come down when you're nice and warm, we'll have some drinks over dinner and discuss the future.' Esme fixed her mum, who was looking on from the front room, with a firm gaze as she finished.

'We've got a lot to discuss and you might need a drink before we're done anyway.' Becky didn't like the look that Esme was giving Aunt Sylvia, she was used to the two of them seeming to keep secrets from Becky and communicate in their own special way sometimes but she'd never seen Esme looking so serious before. Becky traipsed up the stairs and headed for the bathroom.

The cottage was full of wooden interiors, wooden doors, a wooden staircase, wooden floorboards on show all over the house. Most of the walls even had wooden panels on them. Sylvia said it was because it reminded her of home. She much preferred wood to carpet or tiles. She never talked about where exactly home was, it was treated like some magical place where Sylvia was happy and carefree. Becky guessed her aunty was from Greenland or Iceland or someplace like that where there was lots of countryside and greenery. She wasn't very good at geography but to her, these places sounded like the kind of places where you had wood everywhere instead of carpet or tiles.

It was because of the wooden floors that Becky could hear Esme and Sylvia talking in muffled voices downstairs. It was

16

annoying because she could never make out exactly what they were saying, she could only hear the odd word, 'truth' 'right time' 'deserves to know'. She could tell from the tone of their voices that they were talking about her and they were having an argument, just not a loud one, they obviously didn't want Becky to hear what they were saying. Becky undressed, turned the shower on and waited for it to get steaming hot, just the way she liked it.

Becky looked in the mirror while she waited and studied her teeth. She looked at them whenever she got chance, she'd stare at them, wishing they would shrink or fall out, anything but stay how they were. For years she'd dreamt of having false teeth so she could look normal.

One time, when she had just spent the whole of the walk home being teased by Hatty and her friends she had run up to her bedroom with a hammer and chisel with the intention of knocking her teeth out but as she looked in the mirror with chisel held to her front teeth she couldn't bring herself to do it. She'd just gone straight to bed, even more disgusted with herself than usual because now not only was she a freak, she was also a cowardly freak who would have giant teeth her whole life.

She stood under the steaming hot shower for as long as she could stand, closed her eyes and let the water wash over her face. As soon as her eyes were closed all she could see was Hatty Heckstrom and the horrible look in her eyes, full of hate and disgust. She thought back to when she had been truly happy, just a few years ago when her and Hatty had still been friends, when she didn't have a care in the world.

One of Becky's favourite memories was a bonfire night that Sylvia had taken her and Hatty to, they'd eaten toffee apples, candy floss and loads of sweets. She remembered standing with Hatty and getting warm by the bonfire then when the fireworks started Becky and Hatty held hands and looked up in wonder at the amazing fireworks. Every time one shot up in the air, they'd both shout 'ooohhh' then when it banged, they'd shout 'aaaaahhhh'. How could things have changed so much? How could Hatty have changed so much? Becky had no idea but she suspected that it must be her that had changed, that had become unlikeable, even unlovable. She blamed it all on her teeth, she should have smashed them out when she had the chisel to them.

After about twenty-five minutes Becky couldn't stand the hot water anymore, she was starting to feel dizzy and her hands had gone all wrinkly, she got out and got dressed. She couldn't bear to go downstairs yet, she knew she'd have to tell Esme and Sylvia exactly what had happened today and she didn't feel ready. She hated the fact that she brought so much stress into the house but she had no idea what else to do, normally she'd downplay things as much as she could to stop the other two getting upset but she knew she'd reached a tipping point today. Things had to change and they couldn't change unless Sylvia knew exactly what's been going on.

She sat down at her dressing table to dry her hair and try and work out what she would say. She looked at the photos on her mirror, photos of her and Esme on Mam Tor, both of them pretending to jump off into the gravelly drop below. Of her, Esme and Aunt Sylvia standing with Coach Colby outside the entrance to Blue John Cavern, the most famous of cave systems in the Peak District.

Colby worked as a guide in the caverns and had invited the three of them as his guests. They hadn't ended up going into the caves because Aunt Sylvia had a panic attack outside and started crying which started Becky off crying so Esme had to calm them both down and they just ended up going to the Bulls Head for lunch.

Becky looked happy in all the photos. She didn't like to have her photo taken any more because of her teeth so the ones on her mirror were all at least a few years old. She knew it upset Aunt Sylvia that she didn't have any recent photos but she'd run at the sight of a camera these days.

Once her hair was dry she tied it up and went downstairs in her jogging bottoms and hoodie. Esme and Aunt Sylvia were sat at the table already, they each had a glass of red wine, not unusual for Esme but Aunt Sylvia very rarely drank. As Becky went to sit down at the table Esme started to pour her a glass as well.

'No thanks' said Becky, she had only had a drink once, a can of shandy last Christmas at the dance class, Delphine had given it her. Becky felt very grown up until she started getting light headed and feeling sick. She had decided she was definitely too young for drink now.

'Take it' said Esme, holding the full glass out to her, 'you'll need it, we've got a lot to talk about and it's probably best if you're relaxed.

Becky took the glass and had a small sip before putting it down, she tried not to pull a face but couldn't help it, 'lovely' she said, the other two laughed. Aunt Sylvia got up and went into the kitchen to plate up their dinners. She came back carrying two huge plates, each piled high with sausage and mash, Yorkshire pudding, vegetables and gravy. She put the plates in front of Esme and Becky then went to fetch her own. All three of them loved their food and they all tucked in straight away, no-one spoke until they'd all

19

Dan Watford

finished, Sylvia looked like she wanted to talk but was struggling
to find where to start so she looked at Esme and put her head down.
    'Becs' Esme said, 'we just want you to know that whatever
happens we both love you and will support whatever decision you
make.' Becky looked at her confused, waiting for her to carry on.
'Go on mum' Esme said, 'she needs to hear it from you, you were
there.'

CHAPTER 7

Sylvia took a long sip from her wine, put the glass down and coughed. 'You see Becky' she said, 'there's a lot we haven't told you about your parents and some of what we have told you wasn't accurate. But please know that everything we have said and done has been with your best interests at heart, please try and remember that.'

'What are you talking about?' Said Becky, 'what haven't you told me?' She desperately wished Aunt Sylvia would tell her that her parents were on their way to meet with her, that they'd had a change of heart and that they'd take care of everything but she could tell that wasn't where the conversation was going.

'Well' said Sylvia as she looked to Esme for support, Esme nodded to her mother and she carried on. 'It's difficult to know where to start really. The thing is, we're not actually from here, not you, or Esme, or me. We're all from a long way away.'

'Where?' Asked Becky, slightly excited that she was finally going to hear where her Aunt was from.

Sylvia looked Becky straight in the eye so she knew she was serious, 'we're from another planet.'

Becky tried to laugh at her Aunts joke but she didn't think it was funny, besides Aunt Sylvia and Esme weren't laughing either. 'Okay, Aunt Sylvia, good one, that's great, where are we from? Mars?'

'No, we're from a planet called Elfaron. It's in a different universe, far away from here but we managed to get here because someone made a portal and we landed here.'

Becky waited a few seconds for her aunt to carry on but she didn't, so she looked at Esme, Esme nodded. 'It's true, Becky.' She said, 'I know it sounds ridiculous but she's not lying, we really are from a different planet.'

'Don't be ridiculous, haven't I been through enough today having to put up with those idiots at school? Now you're teasing me about other planets, other universes? Stop being daft, now where are we really from?'

'Becky, it's true' Sylvia carried on, 'your mother is still on Elfaron, she was the reason we had to leave, she's the reason we've stayed here for so long. She hasn't just abandoned you, she wants to kill you.'

'She wants to kill me?' Becky screamed. 'Why? What have I done? Is my father still there as well then?'

Sylvia looked over at Esme again and again Esme nodded to her, encouraging her to carry on. 'No' said Sylvia, 'I'm afraid your father, he's, well, he's dead.'

Becky felt like she'd been punched in the stomach, she covered her mouth to stop herself from screaming. Her head was reeling, she couldn't work out why Aunt Sylvia and Esme would be making things like this up, she prayed that it was a practical joke but deep down she knew that from how serious they were acting and the things they were saying were so crazy that they had to be true. She downed the wine and slammed the glass on the table, almost breaking it, Esme got up to pour her a refill.

Becky Bigteeth

'What did he die of?' Becky asked once she'd managed to compose herself.

'He was killed. By your mother.' Said Sylvia.

CHAPTER 8

Becky couldn't help but let out a small scream this time, again she put her hand to her mouth. She started to cry, Esme passed her some tissues.

Sylvia carried on without prompting this time, she felt like now she'd started she just wanted to finish telling the whole story as quickly as she could. Partly to minimise Becky's stress but mainly because she was fed up with keeping it a secret from her niece. It had been eating away at her for years and part of her was slightly relieved to be getting it off her chest.

'You see, the three of us, we're not humans, we're fairies. We took on human form when we got over here so we could fit in and be able to live fairly normal lives, but there are certain aspects of us being fairies that we've been unable to conceal.'

'Wait, wait, wait, wait.' Said Becky, holding her hands up, almost in submission. 'You're now telling me that not only are we from a different planet in a different universe. Not only has my mother killed my father, not only that she now wants to kill me, but also that we're fairies? You've taken your wind up too far, Aunty. I could have believed you up to a point but you're just being ridiculous now, I'm not seven you know, I'm fifteen.'

'Becky' said Esme, 'do you really think we'd wind you up like this knowing how upset you already are about things?' Esme looked pleadingly at Becky, who thought about it for a minute but Sylvia didn't let her reply, she was too keen to carry on.

'That's right, we are fairies, Becky, we live with elves on an island on Elfaron but that island is now being overrun by trolls who your mother, Gelda, has sided with and she's intent on running the elves and fairies as far away from her castle as she can.

Far away from the castle a lot of them grew up in, far away from the homes and lands that have been in their families for generations. And she's doing all this because she's taken up with a troll prince called Aldeese who she's smitten with and never goes anywhere without.'

Sylvia stopped to give Becky some time to catch up with what she was being told but Becky was looking out the kitchen window now, far away into the landscape of the Peak District, she didn't even seem to hear what her aunt was saying, Sylvia carried on anyway.

'You see Becky, there's a magical stone called the Grenchen in the castle on Elfaron that for generations was kept in the highest tower of the castle. There's an ancient prophecy on Elfaron that one day a fairy with magical eyes and teeth will come along and unlock the power of the Grenchen. Legend has it that when the Grenchen's power is unleashed, all evil will be banished from the island and the elves and fairies will be saved from their doom. You're the prophecy, Becky, you're the one that can open the Grenchen and save our people from your mother.'

Becky stared at the two of them. She was still in disbelief, it was ridiculous to think that they were from another planet and weren't even human but somehow, she knew they weren't joking.

Dan Watford

'I need to get some fresh air, this is too much.' Said Becky, she got up from the table and headed straight for the front door, putting her coat on in the hallway. Esme got up to stop her but Sylvia grabbed her arm.

'No' Sylvia said, 'it's fine, let her go, it is a lot to take in. The fresh air will do her good. Go on Becky, we'll be here when you get back.' Sylvia nodded at Becky and tried to force a smile from her but Becky had too much going on in her head to smile.

CHAPTER 9

It was dark out now. Becky was starting to feel like this was the longest day of her life. She left the house and just started walking, she didn't care where she walked, she just needed to clear her head. Her brain was frazzled, she didn't know what to believe or what she was supposed to do next. She decided to head for Mam Tor, it was too dark to ramble over the fields without her head torch but there was a long path leading nearly all the way there which she could stick to, besides, there were no clouds. It was a full moon and there were thousands of stars out so visibility shouldn't be a problem.

Becky looked up to the sky as she walked and imagined being on another planet. What would the sky look like there? Would it still have the sun, the moon and the stars? Her mind wandered to a science class she had with Mr Stephens. She remembered someone once asking him if teleportation was possible, he said he thought it might be but it was still decades away. Yet somehow Becky, Esme and Aunt Sylvia had all teleported here from another planet years ago, how was that even possible?

As she walked past the Bulls Head, she looked through the window and saw the people sat inside enjoying themselves. Drinking beer and wine and eating huge meals without a care in the world. None of them looked like they'd ever had to endure the bullying that Becky had to, none of them looked like they'd grown up with no friends, constantly being told they were freaks and didn't belong. How she envied their normal, happy lives. Why had she not been allowed to lead a normal life? She could cope with not being the most popular person in school but would it have been too much to ask to at least have a couple of friends in her year that would have looked out for her?

Becky carried on up the road, she walked past the visitor's centre, too engrossed in her problems to notice the people in the car park. It wasn't until she got within a few metres of them that she heard a raucous laugh that could only belong to one person, Hatty Heckstrom.

Damn it, thought Becky as she looked at the group and realised Hatty was drinking cider with her friends from school. There were six or seven of them in total, the same group that had been playing football this lunchtime. Hatty and her friends noticed Becky a split second after she had noticed them.

'Look' Wayne Patterson shouted, 'it's the big teeth freak. Hey Bigteeth, what are you doing?'

Becky panicked, there were loads of them, they seemed drunk, it was dark and there were no adults around. She didn't waste another second thinking about her options, she just ran for it, she needed to get away from them as quickly as she could. Hopefully they were too drunk to bother chasing her, they weren't. Unfortunately for Becky they were just drunk enough to cause trouble and just bored enough to chase after Becky to find that trouble, they started to run after her.

'Come on!' screamed Hatty, 'let's get her, first one to trip her up wins.'

Becky Bigteeth

Becky's eyes started to water from running so hard but she kept on, of course, she thought to herself, of course this is happening on this day of all days. She was already a bit wobbly from the wine and with her eyes watering as well it made it nearly impossible for her to keep on the path but somehow, she managed it. Becky cursed herself for running in the wrong direction, she was heading out of the village and away from any possible help, there would be no-one on the empty roads out of the village but there was no way of turning around now.

She could hear them hollering, shouting and laughing, they were definitely closing in on her. Becky thought about heading through the fields, she would definitely know the tracks better than this lot but if they did catch her in the fields there would be no-one anywhere near them. At least if she stayed alongside the road there was an outside chance of a car going past that would help her. She decided to head for the caverns, hoping that they'd give up in a couple of minutes after a bit of fun trying to hunt her down.

'Faster, we've nearly caught her!' Hatty shouted, Becky had nearly reached the steps of the cavern when the wine finally caught up in her, she stumbled and tripped on a stone and went flying, scraping her hands and face on the gravel as she fell.

'She's down' one of the boys shouted. Before Becky could get back to her feet the gang were on her, they formed a circle round her. They were all laughing hysterically but most of them seemed nervous as well, as if they hadn't actually wanted to catch up with her, just chase her for a bit but now they had caught her they seemed unsure what to do.

'Hey, freakshow' said Hatty in between trying to catch her breath. 'What are you running for? Did you really think you'd

29

outrun us? You should have just stayed in the village, now we're really mad.'

'Just leave me alone Hatty.' Said Becky. 'Please, I haven't done anything wrong. I didn't grass on you at school today, I haven't done anything, just leave me alone.'

'Just leave me alone, please!' Wayne Patterson said, mocking Becky in a high pitch voice. The gang all bent double with laughter as several more of them joined in making fun of Becky's pleading as well.

'Why would we leave you alone?' asked Hatty. 'We're bored, we want some fun, there's nothing to do in this boring village.' Hatty looked round at her friends. 'Let's see' she said, 'what could we do for fun?' She started to look round for some inspiration, they were all alone apart from a blue car parked in the layby, it was a boy racer car with a spoiler on the back, Becky thought she recognised the car but didn't have time to pay it much attention, it was weird that it was parked out here at this time of night though.

'I know!' Screamed Hatty as she swayed from side to side, clearly the worse for wear from the cider. 'Let's see how strong your freaky teeth really are, I mean, they look like they could crush boulders, let's see if they can break stones.' Becky looked on incredulously as Hatty bent over to pick up a stone, she nearly fell twice but just caught herself and finally came back up with a big bit of gravel.

'Here' she said, proudly holding the stone out to Becky, 'break this with your teeth.' The rest of the gang cheered and laughed and started chanting 'do it, do it, do it!'

'I can't do that' said Becky, her voice faltering as she looked at Hatty with tears in her eyes.

Becky Bigteeth

'EAT IT!' screamed Hatty, she got right in Becky's face, covering her with spit and the smell of stale cider. Becky looked round the group, praying that she would see a forgiving face but saw none. Everyone just looked fascinated, they couldn't really believe what they were seeing, they knew it was wrong but couldn't look away.

Becky took the stone as Hatty squealed excitedly. She held it in her hand, debating whether she could throw it at Hatty's face and make a run for it again but she knew it was hopeless, they'd be on her in a flash and who knew what they'd do if she made them even more angry.

With no other option she put the stone in her mouth and started moving it around, trying to buy some time and hoping for a miracle. 'There's no way I'm going to be able to break this' she thought to herself, 'I'll break my teeth, maybe that will be a good thing' she decided. She started to chomp down, slowly increasing the pressure on the stone as the onlookers were laughing and sniggering, fixated on what was happening.

'Oi!' a voice shouted from the top of the steps. 'What's going on here?' It was Coach Colby, thank God, thought Becky, I'm saved. She spat the stone out whilst Hatty and her friends looked at Coach Colby, indignant that he'd spoiled their entertainment.

'Well look who it is' said Hatty, staggering towards Colby. 'It's the weird karate man, you two make a good pair, I don't know what's bigger, your hair or her teeth.' Hatty kept walking towards Colby, not realising that her friends had suddenly lost their bravery and seemed to have sobered up all of a sudden. They weren't backing Hatty up, on the contrary, they were backing away.

31

Dan Watford

'Your mouth is bigger than anything round here.' Said Coach Colby, smiling and brushing his bright yellow hair up with his hands. 'You'd better leave, before I do something you'll regret.' He smiled at Hatty again, but it was a cold smile, like he was going to burst into a snarl at any minute.

'We're not scared, are we?' Hatty turned to ask her friends, she suddenly realised they were now about twenty metres behind her, edging back towards the village. Hatty's face dropped, she turned around again and went to push Colby but he side stepped her and she fell into the grass verge. Becky laughed, Hatty turned to look at her and Becky immediately regretted laughing, 'shouldn't have done that', she thought.

'You'll regret this, both of you. You're dead next time I see you, bloody pair of freaks, you deserve each other. You're boring me now, come on guys, we're off.' Said Hatty, trying to save some face.

Once they were gone, Becky burst into tears again, Coach Colby hugged her. 'Come on' he said, 'I'm driving back to the village now, I'll drop you off on my way past. Why are you out so late anyway?'

'You wouldn't believe me if I told you.' Said Becky as she got in the car.

CHAPTER 10

'I'm sorry you have to put up with those idiots.' Colby said as he got in the car. 'I don't know where their parents are or what they're thinking letting their kids go out underage drinking and picking on other kids, they should be ashamed.' Becky didn't say anything, she had only just managed to compose herself and stop crying, she knew if she started talking it would set her off crying again and she didn't like to look weak in front of Coach Colby. He was always telling his students to learn self-discipline, self-confidence and inner strength so she felt that if she started crying in front of him again, she'd be letting him down.

They pulled up outside the house, 'thanks for the lift, Coach' said Becky, getting out of the car. 'I'll be alright from here, I'll see you in class next week.'

'No, it's fine' said Colby, 'I'll pop in, it will be nice to have a chat with the three of you, besides, I've not seen your aunty for a while. She'll enjoy catching up with me.'

'No, honestly, Coach' said Becky, 'it's not a good time, we've got a lot going on and I don't really think any of us are in the mood for company.'

'Nonsense, everyone's in the mood for Coach Colby.' He said as he climbed out of the car.

'I'm back' Becky shouted as they walked in the door. 'I've brought Coach Colby in for a drink, I hope no-one minds.' She secretly hoped someone did mind and would tell him now wasn't a good time, he'd listen to Aunt Sylvia if it came from her. Becky could hear lots of chatter coming from the front room, she was surprised that Esme and Aunt Sylvia would be in such high spirits given the enormity of what had gone on already tonight, but then she realised the voice she could hear belonged to neither Esme or Aunt Sylvia.

She walked in the front room to find Delphine, her dance coach, sat on the two-seater with her feet up, drinking a glass of wine and filling Esme and Aunt Sylvia in on the stresses of being a modern dance coach. Delphine looked delighted to see Becky and jumped up, spilling some wine as she got up, and gave Becky a hug and a kiss on each cheek.

'Becky!' Delphine gasped, 'I'm so glad you've made it back safely, we've been talking about your evening and we were all worried, we were giving it another half hour before going out to try and find you.'

Becky was surprised to hear that Delphine knew about what had been said tonight, surely she couldn't know everything, she'd freak out if she did and not want to see them again, but how much had Aunt Sylvia and Esme told her?

'I hear you've been having a hard time of it lately, I'm really sorry. But fear not, I'm here to help cheer you up. And I see you've brought Colby, if all else fails at least we can just laugh at his hair all night.'

'Hey!' said Colby as he walked in with a beer for him and a glass of wine for Becky. Without saying anything else he walked up to Aunt Sylvia, gave her a kiss on each cheek, then did the same for Esme and then Delphine.

Becky Bigteeth

'Wait' said Becky, taking the glass of wine from Colby. 'Do you two know each other?' she asked.

'Of course we do.' Said Delphine. 'Me and Colby go way back, don't we, Colby? All the way back to Elfaron in fact.'

'What?!' said Becky.

CHAPTER 11

'That's right, Becs' said Delphine with a huge smile on her face. 'We're all from the same planet, we're all outer space weirdos, all five of us. Aren't you glad that we're in this with you?'

Becky wasn't sure if Delphine was being sarcastic or not, she was always this chipper so there was no telling if she really meant it.

Delphine carried on, 'you see, Becs, me and Colby came over with the three of you so we could keep guard over you but also give you guidance and teach you skills. We couldn't exactly come right out and tell you the truth so we had to be careful about how best to do it, that's why we decided to become your teachers.'

'I'm a coach, not a teacher.' Said Colby, interrupting Delphine's flow.

'Okay, dufus' she said. 'Surely it's better to be a teacher than a coach though? Being a teacher means you have actually qualified for something, that you actually have some level of skill. Anyone can be a coach.'

'Not so' said Colby, 'to be a coach means that you have a great deal of discipline and real-life experience in your specialised subject, being a teacher just means you read it in a book. Anyone can read things from a book and pretend to be clever.'

Becky Bigteeth

'Everyone but you, it would seem.' Said Delphine, her white teeth contrasting her exotic skin and shiny dark hair. 'Now, sorry about that, Becs, where was I?'

'You were saying that you two came over to look out for me.' said Becky, keen to hear more from her dance teacher.

'Yes, that's right, ideally we'd have liked a few more to come over and help but we couldn't spare the numbers. A lot had to stay and fight on Elfaron, and besides, we didn't have much time to gather any more troops before we escaped.' Delphine looked over to Aunt Sylvia and they both nodded silently to each other, Sylvia took over from here.

'You see, Becky.' Sylvia said 'after Gelda had your father killed she did a good job of covering it up and making it look like an accident, but there were several elves and fairies who suspected she was involved. Me and my husband Ordren, Esme's father, were certain she'd been behind it.

We were so sure that she'd been involved that we'd started telling others what Gelda was really like and how she had been growing up, always wanting to be the centre of attention and wanting to seize control of The Kingdom. There were whispers that she'd paid someone to kill your father and make it look like an accident. When Gelda got wind of it she had Ordren seized and imprisoned in the dungeons and held me and Esme captive in her quarters.

'Esme was only a toddler so she had no idea what was going on but I knew Gelda, I knew how mad she was and how dangerous she was when she was mad. There was no way she was going to let people get away with spreading stories about her, even if they were her family, especially if they were her family.

Dan Watford

She had a trial for Ordren, he was charged with treason and found guilty, of course he was found guilty, all five judges making the decision were allies of Gelda's. Elder elves that had been on the payroll for years and who had just received huge pay increases from Gelda, they were going to decide whatever she told them to decide. 'She had Ordren executed.' Sylvia stopped talking to gather her thoughts, the thought of her husband's death still upset her, even after all these years, she went over to give Esme a hug too, Esme had heard the story before but hearing it told again was very upsetting for her.

'She had him executed but said she'd show mercy on me seen as I was her flesh and blood. She had her soldiers chop my wings off, I nearly died from my injuries but Delphine saved my life.' Sylvia smiled at Delphine. Becky looked over too, even more confused now, her dance teacher apparently not only knew her family and lived with them on another planet but she was also a life saver.

'Hang on' said Becky, 'so are you a nurse then?' she asked Delphine.

'Not a nurse as such, no, I'm a tooth fairy, hence why I have such magnificent teeth, I've styled them on you. Us tooth fairies have lots of skills and talents, back home, I was the royal tooth fairy. I lived in the castle with you all and was on call almost all the time to deal with any kind of emergency as required, tooth related or not.'

'That's right' said Sylvia 'Delphine's a star back home, everyone admires her for her intelligence, compassion and healing hands.'

38

'And my good looks.' Said Delphine, 'don't forget my good looks.'

'Of course,' said Sylvia, smiling at Delphine. 'And for your good looks. Delphine stopped the bleeding where my wings were cut off and managed to tidy up the wounds a bit so they weren't huge scars. It wasn't totally successful, that's why I have a hunchback and suffer in the cold but it saved my life and I'll always owe her for it, no doubt about it.'

'Things went back to normal after a couple of weeks, I was back on my feet and Gelda made me her personal handmaid as punishment. Me and Esme moved into her living quarters permanently and I was to look after you full time as well because your mother was too busy running The Kingdom.'

'Not long after that, she made the declaration that she was the prophecy and that she had the power to unlock the Grenchen and save the elves. Not that they needed saving from anything at the time but that didn't stop her from staking her claim. All she needed was for her doubters to be silenced and for her looks to be altered somewhat to be able to unlock the Grenchen. She had already achieved the first part, her doubters all went quiet once she'd killed Ordren, for the second part she recruited a sorceress called Velody.'

CHAPTER 12

'The story goes that Velody was a healing fairy living in the castle with her husband and young son. One day her husband and son were heading home from the market when a scaffold that was supporting the extension of the East Tower of Hightown Castle collapsed on them both, killing them instantly.

The king was distraught and offered to help Velody in any way they could but she blamed the king for his vanity in wanting the East Tower extended and swore revenge on all the elves and fairies in The Kingdom. Then she ran off to live in the Woodlands and no-one ever saw her again, until Aldeese brought her back to the castle to help him and Gelda.

'Before Velody left the castle to live in the Woodlands, she knew a little magic which helped her heal the injured and the sick but once she moved to the Woodlands she learned as much magic as she could and practised it daily. Determined that one day her magic would help destroy the elves and fairies to get revenge for her family.

'She was able to use her new found magic to give Gelda bigger teeth, different coloured eyes and even to make a fake Grenchen which they could use to trick the elves and fairies into thinking that it was the real one and that Gelda was the true prophecy.

Becky Bigteeth

'Once everything was in place, Gelda waited for her husband's funeral, your father's funeral.' Sylvia said to Becky, she was aware of how upsetting and confusing all this would be but she decided the best thing to do was to get everything out in the open and deal with all the questions that Becky had later.

'After your father's burial at the sacred ground, the elves and fairies all headed back to the castle courtyard for the traditional feast in honour of their fallen king. Gelda used the feast as her opportunity to reveal herself as the prophecy. She had Velody explain how she was the royal nurse and had been looking after the queen for some time. She said that since the king's passing, she had noticed one or two changes in the queen which didn't seem relevant at the time but now they've all happened together she's realised what it means.

'The crowd were stunned when she said she believes Gelda to be the true prophecy who would save The Kingdom and the future for the elves and fairies. They'd all heard the stories about the prophecy, we were all taught it at school and it was widely thought to be a myth but the people were weak and in need of leadership after the king had died so believed what they wanted to believe. Velody said she would bring the Grenchen in front of Gelda in the courtyard the next day to prove her theory.'

'There was a small group of elves who had been drinking and were feeling brave, they dared to say that they didn't believe her and they should prove it now. This was what Gelda had planned for, Velody went to fetch the fake Grenchen and handed it to the queen. I was on the stage with your mother and knew that it was all fake, I'd heard them planning it for weeks but I was powerless to do anything. Gelda had threatened to have Esme killed if I didn't go along with it and I knew she wasn't bluffing.'

Sylvia had to take a moment to compose herself before carrying on. 'Once your mother had the Grenchen she pretended to be whispering into it and staring at it before smiling and showing it her teeth. Velody used her magic to start the Grenchen off, it went from being a small floating green ball of light to suddenly exploding with light, covering the whole of the courtyard and even the sky above the courtyard. I have to say it was very impressive, if I hadn't known it was fake, I'd have been duped like everyone else was.'

'We weren't all duped' Colby interrupted. 'None of us believed it, did we, Delphine?'

Delphine looked at Colby and shook her head. 'No' she said, 'we knew it was too much of a coincidence that she'd suddenly got these powers now her husband was dead. Besides, we all knew that Velody had only been in the castle for a couple of weeks and all of a sudden, she's the queen's private nurse? No, we knew it wasn't right.'

'But what I don't get.' Said Becky 'Is how come no-one said anything, I mean, surely if you all knew it was rubbish everyone else would have as well. One of you should have said something, surely.' Becky looked accusingly at Delphine and then to Colby. 'I can understand you not saying anything aunty, really I can, you'd just lost your husband and obviously were worried about Esme, but what about you two?' Becky surprised herself that she was actually accusing Colby and Delphine of being cowards but she couldn't understand why nothing was done.

Becky Bigteeth

'You're right, Becky.' Said Delphine, 'we should have done something, said something to someone. Definitely we should have, but at the time we were all very young and everyone had heard the rumours about Ordren. He was very well respected, a powerful and likeable man. If the queen had got away with executing him, she'd have had no problem in silencing us youngsters.'

'We both agree with you, Becky.' Said Colby, taking over from Delphine. 'But what Delphine said is true, we'd have been silenced, possibly even killed like Ordren and back then we didn't have much power, we didn't have many skills. I can't speak for Delphine but I know for me there isn't a day that goes by when I don't think about that ceremony and how someone should have done something. Who knows how things would have turned out but they couldn't have been much worse than they are now. Things will change when we get back. I promise.'

CHAPTER 13

'So, what happened after my mother had opened the fake Grenchen?' Becky asked.

'At first, not much.' Said Sylvia. 'She took her time implementing changes, she's very clever, your mother. She knew if she did too much too soon, the elves and fairies wouldn't have stood for it and would have done something to get rid of her.

'She started changing small things like who was permitted into the castle grounds. It used to have an open gate policy. No-one really caused any trouble amongst the elves and fairies, there were a few trolls in The Kingdom but they kept themselves to themselves and rarely came to the castle. When they did visit the castle, they didn't cause problems so no-one minded.

'But Gelda said they needed more security in the castle grounds so the gate was closed and everyone had to report to the guards if they wanted access. After that she said any trolls who wished to live inside the castle grounds were welcome. This was a big shock for everyone because previously, the trolls had just lived in the Woodlands out of sight, not really wanting to be around the elves and fairies.

'Obviously there were doubts about safety because of how much bigger the trolls are. If they wanted to cause trouble it would take a lot of elves to stop them.' Sylvia looked to Colby, who took his cue to take over the story.

Becky Bigteeth

'The first few months of the trolls living in the castle went smoothly.' He said. 'The trolls pretty much kept themselves to themselves but helped out around the castle, cleaning, building and going out to work in the Woodlands as required. Because they hadn't caused any bother everyone let their guard down and became more relaxed around them. Heck, I even had a beer with some of them from time to time, they didn't say much, but they could drink a lot.

'Then one day Gelda declared that they needed more trolls living in the castle to help with the upkeep of the castle grounds as they were stronger and could work quicker than the elf builders. She asked that fifty elf families give up their lodgings in the castle grounds in exchange for fancy shacks out in the Woodlands. There was no shortage of takers because the shacks in the Woodlands were so much more spacious than the houses in the castle grounds. Elves and fairies with families were keen for their kids to grow up in bigger homes and away from the hustle and bustle of the castle.

'Once the next fifty trolls were moved into the castle, Gelda started making bigger changes. She gave the trolls free run of the most popular taverns and priority shopping at the market. She said this was reward for working so hard keeping the castle up to scratch. All of a sudden elves whose families had drunk in the same taverns for generations found themselves barred from entering because they were now troll only taverns. The trolls could push to the front of the queue for their groceries as well. This disgruntled a lot of us, but still we didn't do anything.' Colby shook his head and stared at the ground in silence, Delphine, seeing Colby's despair, decided to take over the story.

'The elves that had been employed for years taking care of the upkeep of the castle found themselves out of work and had no way of paying their rent to Gelda for their castle lodgings. She offered them a solution, to go to the Wetlands at the very edge of The Kingdom and go and live and work there helping to build boats for her royal fleet. The elves didn't have a choice, if they stayed in the castle they'd be evicted and on the streets with their families. Suddenly, there were hardly any elves or fairies left living in the castle.

'Every day there seemed to be more and more trolls in the castle grounds. They spilled over into the Woodlands, building themselves new shacks once the castle accommodation was full. If they couldn't build a shack fast enough, they'd bully an elf family out of theirs. Threatening violence to the children if the elves and fairies didn't move out. Gelda turned a blind eye, this was what her and Aldeese had wanted all along.

'Some elder elves decided enough was enough and they organised a secret meeting to discuss what was going on and how we could retaliate. It was to be held in one of the Woodland dining shacks, they were huge shacks which could hold hundreds. It was supposed to be a secret but somehow Gelda found out about it and sent twenty trolls to the meeting to stop anyone from entering. They weren't violent but their mere presence was intimidating enough, at this point we realised things were getting very serious, we'd let things go too far.'

CHAPTER 14

Sylvia asked Delphine if she could carry take over and explain to Becky why they had to leave, Delphine was happy for someone else to tell this part of the story.

'A couple of days later,' said Sylvia, 'Gelda announced that all remaining elves and fairies were to leave the castle immediately to make way for more trolls who would help make the castle safer, thus making things safer for everyone. This was such a flimsy reason and everyone saw through it, the elves and fairies were livid, but we'd all let things go too far.

'There weren't enough of us left in the castle to stop her, the trolls heavily outnumbered us. Left with no choice the rest of the elves and fairies had to move out. Some didn't even have anywhere to go to, so had to stay with friends in the Woodlands while they built their own shacks.

'It only took a week from Gelda making the announcement to the last remaining elves and fairies to be forced out. There was no violence but they knew full well there would be if they didn't go. It left just me, you and Esme living inside the castle. Your mother started getting more aggressive towards me, she hated Esme and demanded she be kept out of her sight. Then she started giving you funny looks, Becky.'

'What do you mean funny looks?' Becky asked.

'It changed all the time, one minute she'd look at you like she loved you, then she'd look at you in disgust like she couldn't stand you, then she'd change again and look terrified of you. She never said anything to me but I heard her, Aldeese and Velody talking about you, they'd noticed your different coloured eyes and were always asking if any of your teeth had come through yet. It was obvious they thought you could be the real prophecy.

'That scared your mother more than anything, the thought that you might be the real prophecy and take away from her everything she'd worked so hard for. One day when I was cleaning, I overheard Aldeese and Velody saying that it might be better for everyone if they got rid of you. That way they would be able to relax, knowing that Gelda's lies would never be found out and they could have power forever.'

'From then I knew I had to get you to safety but I had no idea where we'd go or how we'd get away. That's where Delphine came in.' Sylvia nodded towards Delphine and smiled at her, Delphine returned her smile with a dazzling smile with all her huge teeth on show, Becky wondered how Delphine's teeth could look so big yet so perfect when her own looked so big and ugly.

'As we said, Delphine was the royal tooth fairy. Her family had been looking after our family for generations and I'd known Delphine all my life. I've seen her grow, I've watched her learn everything from her mother and eventually take over from her mother to look after us all. I knew if I could trust one person in The Kingdom it was Delphine, and I knew she had friends who would be able to help us if needed.'

'What could her friends do though if Gelda had so many trolls around?' Becky asked, looking from her aunty then to Delphine.

'Well' Delphine said, 'me and Colby are in a gang you see.' Delphine smiled and looked over at Colby who smiled as well.

'Gang?' Colby shouted, still smiling, 'I keep telling you, Ergo kept telling you, everyone kept telling you, we're not a gang. We're a crew, we're the Ergo Six Crew, not the Ergo Six Gang.'

'What's the Ergo Six Crew?' Becky asked, she was starting to laugh, thinking it sounded like such a daft name.

'Oh Becky,' said Delphine, 'the Ergo Six Crew are the finest group of warriors in the entire Kingdom. There's six of us and we have a leader, a giant called Ergo.'

'A giant?!' Becky exclaimed. 'You're kidding.'

'No way. We're not kidding.' Said Colby. 'Ergo's amazing. Stronger than an elephant, bigger than anyone you've ever seen and smarter than...' Colby stopped to think for a second, 'well, okay, he's not that smart, but he's dead big and really strong, you'll be very impressed when you meet him.'

Colby carried on, 'then there's Tendril, another fairy, like Delphine. Tendril is fierce, fast and fantastic. There's also Stanton and Martinez. Stanton is an inventor elf, he's very smart. He's making loads of magic animals to help us win the war. Martinez is one of a kind. Half elf, half something else. No-one's worked out what his other half is yet but he's a great fighter and a scary guy. We're glad Martinez is on our side.'

'That's great, Colby.' Sylvia said, 'but can I please finish telling my part?' She was aware she was probably sounding rude but she just wanted to get everything out so she could relax, she'd been keeping secrets for far too long. Colby smiled and nodded, and let her carry on.

Dan Watford

'So, I went to see Delphine and told her about my concerns for you. She took them really seriously and said she wasn't surprised that Gelda was worried. She agreed that we needed to act straightaway, so we sat down and came up with a plan.'

CHAPTER 15

'As luck would have it, Gelda had mentioned that she was going away the next day and would be gone for two days. This wasn't unusual, she regularly had trips away. Her, Aldeese and Velody were the only ones who went and they were always really secretive about where they were going and what they were doing. I never even saw them leave.

'We made plans to meet up the next night once they'd gone, it was pretty easy really. There's a secret tunnel in the dungeons of the castle which not many people knew about. It goes right underneath the moat, and comes out deep in The Woodlands. We arranged to meet at the tunnel exit the next night.

'The only trouble I had was getting into the dungeons. There were trolls posted down there but because there were no prisoners, they were very relaxed about their duties. I managed to sneak past them with you two in tow and crept through the tunnel to meet Colby and Delphine.'

'That's right,' said Delphine, her chirpiness made both Esme and Becky jump, they'd been deep in concentration listening to Sylvia. Esme was just as enthralled as Becky was, although she'd heard snippets of this story before she hadn't heard it in this much detail.

Delphine carried on with the story, 'once you three were with us we all climbed onto Blaze, my flying horse, and we flew far away, over The Woodlands and The Swamplands and deep into The Wastelands. The Wastelands are almost at the edge of Elfaron, only The Wetlands stand between them and the Santurn Sea.

'We flew to the caves of the Wastelands, far away from where any trolls ever ventured, and landed outside the caves. I said a long goodbye to my good friend Blaze, he'd been with me for years but we obviously couldn't bring a flying horse with us, it would have stood out a bit! So, he flew back to be with the rest of the Six Crew, whilst we went into the caves, I worked my magic and brought us here.'

'Worked your magic?!' Becky asked, this was all getting more and more outrageous by the minute. 'What magic?'

'Well, I'm not just a tooth fairy.' Said Delphine, 'I also practised a lot of magic, I learned a lot from Tendril and taught myself a lot from the old books as well. Don't get me wrong, I'm nowhere near as powerful as Velody, neither is Tendril, but we are both pretty handy to have around.'

'My speciality was creating portals. Once we were inside the caves, I managed to make a portal to get us off Elfaron and get you to safety. Unfortunately, my magic isn't strong enough to be able to control where the portal would bring us out. It could have taken us anywhere but we were willing to take the gamble, or, at least, Colby was.' Delphine smiled and looked over at Colby.

'That's right,' he said, smiling, 'although our brave warrior Delphine did well making the portal, she wasn't quite brave enough to try it herself and see where it would come out. Were you Delphine?'

'Well, not quite, no. I don't like water you see, Becky, I'm not a very good swimmer and I was worried the portal would have sent us out in the middle of the sea somewhere. So, Colby went first to check out where it went.' Delphine looked over at Colby to carry on.

'That's right,' he said, puffing up his chest, 'I was brave enough, luckily for you lot.' He smiled over at the others. 'The portal came out in a dark cave, I waited there for five minutes to see if anything would happen. When it didn't, I went back through to tell you all it was safe. We all came back through and rested in the cave for a bit, going through a portal can be quite tiring you see.' Colby looked at Becky, who just nodded, wanting him to carry on.

'Once we'd had a bit of rest I looked after you three while Delphine went to scope out the new neighbourhood.' Colby nodded over to Delphine and smiled.

'It was still dark when I left the cave.' Delphine said. 'And it seemed like we'd landed in the middle of nowhere but I eventually saw the lights and walked towards the village, being careful not to be seen obviously.' Delphine smiled at Becky, 'believe it or not we don't actually look like this back home, I'd have stood out a mile if I'd have just walked into the village in full on fairy mode.'

'Fairy mode?' Said Becky, 'so, what do we really look like?'

Delphine, Sylvia and Colby all looked at each other and burst out laughing. 'You wouldn't believe me if I told you!' Delphine said. 'You'll have to wait until we're back home, but let's just say we're a bit shorter and us fairies have a few more wings.'

'So I saw a few humans walking in the village. I made sure I memorised all their features so I could use the transforming spell, then I ran back to the cave. We all slept in the cave that night then in the morning I performed the transforming spell on us all.

The spell worked great, we all fitted in perfectly, the only thing it didn't change were your eyes Becky but that didn't matter because people here can have different coloured eyes as well. But then your teeth came through, we hadn't thought of them and we couldn't do anything about it once they started growing.'

'So, what happened back home after we'd left? Do you even know? Have you been able to go back?' Becky asked, looking round at Sylvia, then Colby then Delphine.

'No dear' said Sylvia, 'we've never been able to go back, we were worried it would compromise the portal and if anything happened to that we wouldn't be able to get you back.

'But what if I don't want to go back?' Becky asked.

'That's your decision' said Colby, 'but you need to know what's been happening back home, and what will happen if you don't go back.' He looked at Delphine, then back to Becky, 'we know this is a lot to take in, Becky but trust me, our entire future and the future of our family and friends depend on you.'

Becky stared at Colby, still half expecting this to be a big wind up, she had no idea what she should say, fortunately, Sylvia broke the silence. 'Come on' she said, grabbing Becky and Esme by the hand and leading them into the living room, 'there's something you need to see.'

CHAPTER 16

The five of them sat round the fire in the living room. The fire was roaring away as it always was. It was as much a constant in Becky's life as the bullying was. She loved the smell of the fire, she always felt safe when she could smell the fire and hear the crackling of the logs.

'Becky' Aunt Sylvia said, 'the fire does make my back more relaxed but that's not the only reason I keep it in constantly, it also tells me what's going on back home.' Sylvia looked at Delphine and Colby and laughed, 'shall we?' she asked them.

Without answering, Delphine stood up and put her hand in her pocket, pulling out a small silver pouch, she undid the drawstring, put her hand inside and came out with a small handful of powder. 'Watch this, Becky' she said and threw the powder onto the fire.

Nothing happened at first, then, after a few seconds the fire grew and became more intense. Becky was sat next to Esme on the sofa, they were holding hands, Becky gripped Esme's hand as tightly as she could. They watched as the fire started turning different colours, from orange, to red, then blue, then green before settling down to a faint red glow. Noises started coming from the fire, they reminded Becky of wildlife documentaries in the jungle, there was whistling, screeching, hollering and the sound of footsteps.

Dan Watford

The colours from the fire lit up the front room, Becky and Esme both stared, mesmerised, as they started to see shapes forming in the fire.

'We're looking through the eyes of my pet bird, Janstel.' Said Aunt Sylvia, 'she's a very special bird and with the help of a bit of fairy magic she's able to fly all over The Kingdom and show me everything that she can see.'

Becky was listening to her aunty but was too enthralled with the fire to take her eyes off it. Sylvia carried on, 'it used to be that everything she showed us was pretty normal, but these last few months.' Sylvia paused and looked at Colby and Delphine, unsure of how to continue. 'Well, these last few months have been a bit worrying.'

The picture in the fire became clearer and clearer until it was almost as if someone was projecting a film into it. It was very dark but they could see trees for miles, the jungle noises started to be drowned out by the sound of running water. The picture moved as Janstel moved his head to show a waterfall right near the tree he was perched on top of. The waterfall fed into a huge lake in a clearing in the jungle. Throughout the jungle, small strands of smoke reached up through the trees as if there were small campfires every half mile or so.

Becky and Esme jumped as the picture suddenly started moving, Janstel had flown off his perch in the tree and was flying above the trees and heading towards more open land. The picture moved faster and faster as Janstel picked up speed. It was difficult to spot everything at this speed but Becky could swear she saw small armies of green soldiers every so often. Janstel slowed down and it became easier to see. There were swamps, lots of swamps, all over the place. Built around the swamps were wooden huts on legs to keep them above the waterline.

It was getting lighter the further Janstel flew, the swamps started to make way to more solid ground. It began to get much lighter. Becky couldn't understand how it could suddenly go from dark to light, unless Janstel had travelled much further than it seemed. The trees were all behind them now and it appeared they were flying over a desert. There was sand everywhere, and no sign of life out there other than a lot of patches of cactus trees. They were the biggest cactus Becky had ever seen. Janstel kept flying until he came to a rocky mountain range which seemed to wall off the desert. He flew to the top of the highest mountain and sat on top, looking all around him.

On the far side of the mountains was the sea, Becky squinted her eyes and focussed as hard as she could to see if she could see any other land in the sea but it was no good, it looked like the sea went on forever. There was a harbour not too far from the mountains, several ships were being built in the harbour, the ship workers seemed to be hard at work, not noticing or caring that they were being spied on by a magic bird who was transmitting their images to a foreign planet.

All of a sudden Janstel was up and flying again, this time faster than ever and back the way he had come. Back across the barren desert, over the swamps and over the forests. The further he went, the darker it became. Again, they could make out crowds of people in the swamps and the forests. Suddenly the forest started to go uphill, he flew over the waterfall he was perched on earlier and went higher and higher up the hill.

Dan Watford

As he looked up, the five spectators could see what he was seeing and flying towards. A huge castle, built on top of the highest mountain in the land. Weirdly, although it was dark leading all the way up to it, somehow the castle was in broad daylight and whilst the wooded area all around it was pouring with rain the castle looked bone dry.

It had a tower in each corner, three towers were very big but the fourth tower was huge, it must have been a hundred metres higher than the other towers and instead of turrets like the other towers had the top of the fourth tower was a huge glass dome.

CHAPTER 17

Janstel landed on one of the smaller towers and stood looking out over the land outside the castle. Becky and Esme screeched as they saw what appeared to be giant spiders so big they each had two people riding on their backs. The spiders seemed to be everywhere, some were walking round and round the castle as if guarding it whilst others were being ridden out into the woods by the people on their backs.

The castle was surrounded by a dark and cold looking moat, the water was too murky to make out what was swimming inside but dark moving shadows suggested that whatever was swimming in there was both gigantic and dangerous. It was doubtful there would be too many people queueing up to even stand near the moat, let alone swim in it to get to the castle.

Janstel turned away from the lands outside the castle and turned his attention to inside the castle, giving Becky and Esme their first glimpse of the inside of the castle that had seemingly already played such a big part in their lives.

It was similar to the castles they'd seen on the telly hundreds of times before. It had a courtyard with lots of seating, lots of shops and pubs. There were hundreds of people milling about inside, well, they weren't really people, they were trolls.

There were trolls with green skin, big heads, broad shoulders and menacing demeanours. Some were dressed in everyday clothing, old fashioned clothing, but everyday clothing nonetheless. Others, the majority in fact, were dressed as soldiers and they had the weapons to prove it. There were archers with bows and arrows slung over their shoulders, and swordsman with shiny swords and big shields. Becky even saw one playing the trumpet, although it appeared to be for entertainment rather than to give the signal of an impending battle.

Just then they all stopped, soldiers and civilians alike, and stood to attention, leaving a wide walkway between them. The trolls all started saluting as three figures on horseback rode by them.

The first of the three was a slim, fairly young-looking troll wearing a very smart black jacket with shiny brass buttons done all the way up to the top. He was unarmed on the horse but had the air of someone confident enough to not be challenged by anyone, Becky thought he looked dangerous enough without having any weapons as well.

Behind him followed a beautiful lady, riding a magnificent white horse. She had long golden hair which flowed over her shoulders and down her back. She was wearing a small, tidy crown which had a glowing green ball at the front, the gold crown matched her golden hair perfectly. Becky focussed in harder to try and see her eyes, she couldn't be sure but it seemed like she had one green eye and one blue eye, just like her.

As she was leaning in to see better, the lady suddenly smiled, showing off huge, magnificent teeth. They weren't quite as big as Becky's teeth, but they were still much bigger than average, yet somehow, they seemed to fit the lady's face perfectly. Becky wished her teeth looked that good, she'd be proud to have giant teeth if hers looked like that.

'That must be my mother' thought Becky, she suddenly felt very sick and grabbed Esme's hand even harder. Before today she'd been told that her mother had abandoned her and didn't want anything to do with her. Now she'd learned that her mother was actually a queen on a distant planet, wasn't even human and rather than abandon her, she actually wanted to kill her.

Becky had to fight the urge to run out of the room and not come back, she couldn't believe that the beautiful lady she was watching in the fire could possibly be so evil as to have killed her father and want her dead. She shut her eyes tight for a few seconds, hoping things would become clearer. They didn't.

Behind her mother was an older looking lady, dressed all in black and riding a black horse. The only bit of colour about her was a glowing green orb on the end of a stick she was carrying, it matched the green ball in her mother's crown. The stick reminded Becky of a witch's wand, in fact, the more she looked at the lady at the back the more she resembled a witch. Her back was hunched over, her hands were clenched tightly, one around the wand, the other around the reigns of the horse. And Becky couldn't be entirely sure because of how far away Janstel was sat but she was pretty certain she could see a wart on the end of her nose.

'Thanks, Janstel' said Aunt Sylvia, 'that's enough.' And with that the picture in the fire disappeared and they were suddenly just staring into a normal fireplace.

Dan Watford

CHAPTER 18

'That, dear Becky' said Delphine 'is our homeland, Elfaron. Or The Kingdom, as we like to call it. What do you think?' Delphine smiled at Becky, feeling sure that Becky would be just as excited about it as she was. Delphine was nothing, if not positive.

Becky, unable to think of anything suitable to say decided to say nothing, she was still too busy running things through her mind. Could this be a joke the others were playing on her? She felt not, she knew that she'd already seen things tonight that couldn't be answered away as just a joke. The magic fire, for example, how could they have done that if it wasn't real? No, not a joke, but what do they want from me? This is too much to take.

Colby spoke up for her. 'I'm sure Becky just needs a bit of time to let things sink in, right, Becky?' Becky nodded. 'Why don't we go and sit outside?' Colby asked. 'The fresh air will do us good, besides, staring into the fire has made my eyes funny.' He got up to go outside, the others followed suit.

'I'll be out in a minute.' Said Becky, heading upstairs, 'I'm just going to the toilet.' She ran up the stairs, straight into the bathroom and shut the door behind her. As soon as she was in the bathroom she collapsed to the floor, all these revelations had taken it out of her. She sat on the floor and started to cry, she was mourning her father, devastated about her mother and overwhelmed with everything she'd discovered today.

She sat on the floor for a long time, trying to stop herself crying. She was fed up with herself for always crying, it seemed to be all she did. She couldn't imagine anyone else her age having things as tough as she was. What with all the bullying and her giant teeth. But now to top it off, she had to decide whether to stay here in Castleton, where she'd never really felt she'd fitted in, or go home to her own planet and help her fellow elves and fairies fight off her evil mother. It was too much for her brain to take, she fell asleep.

As she slept, she had vivid dreams, of elves, fairies, flying horses, giant spiders and trolls. She dreamt she was a cat inside the castle grounds, watching everyone trundle by. There were trolls everywhere, drinking outside the taverns, buying and selling at the marketplace and heading off in all directions carrying out all sorts of errands.

Suddenly she heard a commotion, still in cat form she leapt behind a nearby bin. She stuck her head out to see what was happening, and saw three dogs riding on horseback. Surely there couldn't really be dogs that could ride horses, but she shook her head and the dogs stayed on the horses. The horses were slowly walking by, the trolls stopping and bowing their heads to the three dogs as they went.

Just as the horses were passing the bin that Becky the cat was hiding behind, the big green dog at the front jumped down and threw the bin to one side. Becky froze on the spot, not sure where to go or what to do, before she had made a decision the dog grabbed her with its two front paws, it seized her by the neck and pinned her to the ground.

Then the second dog jumped down, it was a scruffy, old dog with a wiry black coat. It sniffed Becky's face and growled a wheezy, high pitched growl. The third dog jumped down, it was a splendid dog with a shiny, immaculately groomed, yellow mane. Becky tried to scream as it got closer but all she could manage was a miaow, what was happening? She thought, 'why am I a bloody cat?' She tried screaming again, but again it did no good, she could only manage cat noises. She watched on in terror as the lovely looking dog, which she somehow knew to be the most terrible of the three got closer. Just then, it spoke to her, not in a dog voice but in a wonderful, gentle, caring, female voice.

'Becky' the dog said, 'my darling, I knew you'd come home to me. They told me I was being silly and should forget all about you, but how could I? You're my precious little girl, thank goodness you've manage to get away from your horrible aunty. Come and give your mother a kiss.' The dog started to transform into a beautiful lady, it wasn't the same lady that Becky had seen in the fire earlier, yet somehow, she knew it was her mother.

Gelda leaned in closer to Becky and smiled, showing off her magnificent, shiny, white teeth, Becky was mesmerised. But as Gelda got in closer to give her daughter a kiss, Becky noticed blood coming out of her mother's mouth. It was just a small spot at first, then more and more drops started to run down her teeth until eventually she looked like a werewolf. Becky screamed as her mother got closer, she felt for sure she was going to tear her throat out. She managed to scream like a human rather than a cat and suddenly she could hear banging and someone shouting her name.

'Becky! Becky!' it was Colby, just outside the bathroom door, he was banging on it as hard as he could. Becky woke up, still terrified from her dream and screamed again. The door burst open as the lock went flying and Delphine ran to Becky and hugged her, shushing and whispering into her ear that everything was going to be okay, it was just a bad dream. Becky was still shaking but managed to calm down after a few minutes.

'I can't go back' she said after she'd calmed down. 'My mother, she's terrifying, she'll kill me, I know she will, I can't go back, you can't make me.' She shouted to the others, they were all stood in the bathroom now, she looked at each of them, one after the other. 'You'll all just have to go back without me, what good would I be anyway? I'm only a little girl, I get bullied by other kids, I'd be useless against trolls.'

'No, you wouldn't, Becky.' Said Delphine as gently as she could. 'You're the chosen one, the prophecy that will save our people, without you we'd all be useless, but with you, we'll all be saved.'

'She's right, Becky' said Colby 'you're our princess, our leader, our warrior.'

'Warrior', Becky thought, she liked the sound of that, she didn't believe it for one second, but she certainly liked the sound of it.

Once everyone's heartbeats had gone back to normal, they all started to go downstairs so they could go back outside and relax. Becky grabbed Esme's sleeve just as she was stepping off the landing, 'hang on, Esme' she said, 'can we talk, just me and you, in our bedroom?'

'Sure' said Esme as she gave her cousin a warm, reassuring smile.

CHAPTER 19

Becky shut the door behind them to make sure they couldn't be heard then followed Esme's lead by sitting on the edge of her bed. 'What do you make of all this Esme? I mean, I know you knew more than me, I'd always thought you and your mum were talking about things behind my back, at least now I know what you were talking about. But what do you think I should do? It's all just so weird.'

'Trust me Becky,' said Esme, 'no-one thinks it's weirder than I do. When my mum first started telling me stuff I used to think she was mad, not mad in a good way but proper mad, up the wall, lock you up mad. But then she introduced me to Colby and Delphine and they were the coolest people I'd ever met so when they started saying the same thing, I started to believe them.'

'How long have you known for?' Becky asked, she was starting to get annoyed that her cousin knew all this and hadn't said anything, they were supposed to be best friends, how could she keep a secret like that?

'Oh, about a year.' Esme said, 'I really wanted to tell you, Becs, believe me I did. I was always arguing with mum saying we should tell you but she said it wasn't my decision to make, it's up to Colby and Delphine, they're your special guardians.'

Becky suddenly started to feel bad for Esme, now she thought about it she had always wondered why there was tension between

Esme and Aunt Sylvia when she walked in the room sometimes. This must have been hard on her cousin who obviously felt powerless to say anything to her. 'Well, what do you think we should do?' Becky asked.

'It's obvious isn't it? We should go, what's here for us anyway, come on, Becs, you of all people must know we don't really fit in around here. Wouldn't you be happier amongst your own people? People who won't judge you or make horrible comments or try and make your life miserable?'

'But this is our home.' Becky said, to be truthful she was hoping Esme would have been a bit less decisive about things. This was a huge, irreversible decision to make and it felt weird that there was no alternative.

'It's where we live' said Esme, 'but it's not home, it never has been. Do you think home is somewhere where you're picked on for being different, where you can't walk down the street without fear of being bullied? Or is home somewhere you're completely comfortable and accepted for who you are, loved for who you are?'

'How do you know it will be like that?' Becky asked.

'How could it not be, if everyone's like Colby and Delphine? Besides, you heard them in there.' She said, pointing towards the door, 'you're the chosen one, the princess' Esme started to laugh and imitate Colby, 'you're a Warrior!' The girls burst out laughing at Esme's impression, the tension left the room again and they were back to best friends, just like that.

Becky went serious again for a second, 'but, what if my mother tries to hurt me?' She asked.

Esme grabbed Becky's hands and held them tightly, 'don't worry, Becs' she said, 'I won't let anything happen to you, I promise.'

Dan Watford

CHAPTER 20

The two cousins made their way down the stairs and outside where Colby, Delphine and Aunt Sylvia were sat on the patio chairs. They'd all topped up their wine and Colby and Delphine had both lit cigars. To Becky and Esme's amazement, Delphine was blowing smoke rings while Sylvia cheered her on, Colby was trying to as well but not having much success.

'Heyyyyy.' Said Delphine when she saw the girls, 'sooooo' she carried on, clearly worse for wear. 'What's crackalacking, Becky? Are you going to come home and fight with us or are you going to stay here and be miserable?'

'Delphine!' said Colby, he was trying to be serious but ended up bursting out laughing. For some reason his laughter was contagious, Delphine joined in first, followed by Aunt Sylvia, Becky and Esme soon followed suit and it was a long time before they regained their composure.

'How could I miss out on the fun?' said Becky when the laughter had died down.

'So, you mean, you'll come back with us?' Asked Aunt Sylvia, 'are you sure that's what you want dear?'

Becky looked at Esme, who shrugged her shoulders and smiled. 'Yes' Becky said, 'I'm sure, there's nothing for me here anyway.'

The group all cheered, not caring about waking up the neighbours, they all stood up and hugged in a circle.

'This is great news.' Said Colby, 'cigars all round' he reached into his jacket pocket to bring out his cigar tin but was thwarted by Aunt Sylvia.

'No, Colby' she said, 'it's a nice gesture but they're too young for cigars, besides, if they taste like they smell, they'll be horrible.'

Colby feigned offense and sat back down to try smoke rings again.

'So, when do we leave?' Asked Esme.

'Tomorrow night' said Delphine, 'come on, let's go back inside, have one last drink then it's time we all went to bed, we need to pack tomorrow and have plenty of energy for the journey.

Delphine put her cigar in the ashtray while Colby stubbed his out and put it back in his tin, he didn't believe in wasting cigars. Then they all went inside, Becky's head was too fuzzy for another wine so she and Esme had a hot chocolate while the other three polished off the Zinfandel. This whole day had been a whirlwind for Becky, so much had happened and so many revelations had been revealed that she couldn't get her head round it, could she really be leaving forever tomorrow?

She knew it had to be true but it still felt surreal. She couldn't imagine leaving Castleton, this had always been her home and even though a lot of the people here didn't like her she loved the place. It was beautiful and there were some really nice people around as well, it's just a shame they were so outnumbered.

It was well past midnight when Colby and Delphine left. Becky, Esme and Aunt Sylvia all went straight up to bed once they'd gone. Becky was asleep as soon as her head hit the pillow. If she dreamt tonight, she couldn't remember by the morning.

CHAPTER 21

Becky woke up the next morning with a sore head and a dry throat. Her lip was swollen where Hatty had kicked the ball in her face and her hands and knees were grazed from when she fell over. Despite all this Becky felt wonderful, the whole thing still seemed surreal to her as she opened her curtains and looked out at the other kids walking to school. They all had their heads down, walking as slowly as possible, just waiting for the end of the school day.

She couldn't help but wonder what life was going to be like on Elfaron. Would there still be school? Would there still be bullies? Would there still be people that were so miserable with their own lives that they made it their mission in life to try and make everyone else as miserable as them? Becky hoped not, besides, she was a princess where she was going, if she didn't like things there she could just change the rules.

The smell of one of Aunt Sylvia's fry ups drifted upstairs to her bedroom. Fry ups were only for special occasions and they were always delicious. She ran downstairs without brushing her teeth to see if it was ready yet.

'Good morning, my darling.' Said Aunt Sylvia, she looked younger than Becky had ever seen her before, like the weight of the world had been lifted from her, allowing her to stand straighter than usual and smile away her frowns.

'Morning, Aunty' said Becky, 'this smells amazing, it must have taken you ages. How long have you been up?'

'Oh, a long time, my dear. Who needs sleep when we're going home?'

'You still need sleep Aunty. We've got a long day of packing, then a long journey ahead.'

'My dear, I've been sleeping for fifteen years, I've had enough sleep to last me a lifetime. Now I just want to go home and fight to take back our kingdom.'

Becky didn't say anything else about sleep, she was just glad to see her Aunty looking so refreshed and happy. She could hear banging in the front room. She went in and found Esme stood in the middle of the room with what looked like her entire earthly possessions laid out on the floor. She'd made three different piles, each one bigger than the next and none of them looked like they would fit in her rucksack.

'Hi, Esme, how's it going?' Becky asked, still with a huge smile on her face.

'Hey, Becs. Not bad, but I just can't whittle stuff down enough to get it all to fit. There's just too much stuff I need to take.' Becky looked at the piles on the floor, there really was stuff everywhere.

'Are you sure you need so many batteries?' She asked, 'and three pairs of shoes? Surely you could make do with a pair of trainers. Deep heat? You're taking deep heat?'

'Of course I am, we'll be walking a long way, what will I do if I sprain my ankle or something?'

Becky Bigteeth

'Esme, do you mean to tell me that Delphine can create a magic portal that can teleport us from one planet to another but she can't work a bit of magic on a sprained ankle?'

'You're right, I hadn't thought of that. I think I'll leave this cough syrup as well then.'

'Jesus.' Said Becky, she decided she'd do a bit of packing whilst waiting for breakfast to be served. She didn't take long, there wasn't much she was sentimental about in Castleton, apart from a few photos of the three of them. She packed a spare pair of clothes, her anorak, a whistle and a head torch. Four minutes later she was finished, just in time for Aunt Sylvia to call her down for breakfast.

They all ate in silence, going back for seconds, even thirds until there was no food left. They let their breakfast settle while Aunt Sylvia phoned Becky's school to tell them she wouldn't be in today. She said she was too upset about the football incident and wanted to stay off for the day, and if the school didn't like it, that was their problem. Once that was done the three of them decided to go for one last walk over Mam Tor, their favourite place on Earth. They would all miss the walks on Mam Tor, especially standing on the edge looking out over the beautiful Peak District.

It chucked it down while they were out so they didn't hang around, just a quick stomp up to the top while they stood on the edge with their arms around each other and allowed themselves to get upset for the things they'd miss. Then it was straight back down to the house where they could all get warm and dry, no-one wanted the sniffles for their long journey.

Just as the clock struck five, the three of them were sat on the sofa, tapping their feet and inspecting their nails when Colby and Delphine walked in, they didn't bother knocking.

'Hi de hi' said Colby even more chirpy than usual. 'Who's ready to go travelling to a different planet? We're all too good for this world anyway.'

'Right.' Said Delphine, clapping her hands together. She seemed a lot more serious than usual. 'Have you all got rid of as many fairy items as you can?' She asked them, Becky was confused, she didn't know what fairy items were, let alone how to get rid of them, or even if they had them. Delphine took the silence as a positive answer. 'Great' she said, 'I know we're never coming back but there's no point in alerting people about our real selves is there? Mobiles, have you all left your mobiles here?' Becky shook her head, so did Esme, neither of them could ever remember leaving the house without their mobiles, it seemed almost criminal to leave them behind.

'Bloody hell girls' said Delphine, 'do you want the police tracing the signal to the caves, finding the portal and ending up on Elfaron?' she asked. 'Besides, what are you going to do with them? There's no mobile signal on Elfaron you know, you'd just end up carrying about little chunks of plastic for no reason. Go and leave them upstairs.'

Becky and Esme did as they were told and left them on their beds. When they ran downstairs, they found Colby, Delphine and Sylvia all stood in a circle, hugging. The two girls joined them so they were stood in a circle in the middle of the front room, they hugged tighter and tighter, until Delphine broke them up.

'Come on, guys, it will soon be dark, we can go now.' Delphine said.

Sylvia locked the door behind her and put her key in her pocket, 'what are you going to do with that?' Esme asked her.

74

Becky Bigteeth

'Oh, I know it's useless to us now but I'd like to keep it as a souvenir, we've been really happy in this house most of the time and I've loved watching you two grow up, I'll hang it in my next house as a reminder.'

CHAPTER 22

The five of them quickly and quietly walked out of Castleton for the final time, Becky was dreading bumping into Hatty or her friends on the way out but it was uneventful, they passed a few people but no-one they knew and no suspicions were raised.

Colby had been last on shift at Blue John Cavern so he knew they wouldn't have to worry about any other guides seeing them and stopping them, or even worse, following them.

It was a cloudless night with a full moon meaning they didn't need their torches on the walk to the caves, but once they were in the caves everyone turned their headtorches on. Colby led the way and they walked down, down, down, further and further into the caves.

They'd been walking for a good couple of minutes when Colby turned around to the others, 'right, time to start climbing' he said. And with that he started to clamber up the wall, Sylvia followed him with Esme and Becky close behind and Delphine bringing up the rear. It soon became very clear that Sylvia had not been doing enough exercise the last couple of years. She was soon struggling to climb up, meaning Colby had to regularly turn back and give her a helping hand.

What should have taken five minutes to climb up to the ledge leading to the portal ended up taking twenty-five minutes but none of them complained. They all encouraged and helped out Sylvia as much as they could. Eventually they got to the ledge and Colby leant over the edge to help them all up, one by one.

When they were all on the ledge they rested for a couple of minutes before they headed down a small, pitch black passageway. Colby had to move several big rocks out of the way as they went. 'We put these in the way to stop anyone from finding the portal.' Delphine said as she helped Colby with some of the bigger rocks.

A few minutes further down the tunnel they started to see a light. At first it was a dim glow but the closer they got the brighter it got until they came to a small hole that looked just big enough for them to fit through. It was so bright in the hole that Becky had to look away to stop it hurting her eyes.

Delphine crouched down first and climbed through the hole, then held her hand out to help the others. Becky followed behind Esme. As she climbed through the hole she saw what looked like a patch of floating water, rippling on the surface and reflecting their faces as they looked into it.

'There it is' said Delphine, 'the portal back to Elfaron, somehow, it's stood there for fifteen years undetected by humans despite them regularly exploring these caves, we've been very lucky. Now, who wants to go first?' She asked, clapping her hands together for effect.

'I'll go' said Colby, 'if there's anything on the other side we'd rather not meet I'll do my best to get back through to warn you. If I don't come back within two minutes just assume everything is safe and follow me through.' He looked at Delphine and nodded, she smiled back at him, they were all unsure of what they might find the other side or even if they could get back but they all tried to act cool so Becky wouldn't panic.

'But what if there's something there that hurts you, or…. kills you?' Becky asked, not really wanting to know the answer.

'Well, if it's good enough to get me it will definitely get you lot.' He said, trying to lighten the mood. 'Good luck.' He winked at Becky as he ran into the portal.

The wait was the longest two minutes of all their lives. In reality they only waited fifty seconds before Delphine lost her nerve and said they'd waited long enough. Esme insisted on going next, Becky wanted to go at the same time but Delphine made her wait thirty seconds in case they injured each other on the way through. It reminded Becky of queueing for the flume at the swimming pool.

Eventually, Delphine said she could go through, Becky stood up, patted herself down and nodded at Sylvia and Delphine. 'Don't worry, Becs, you'll be fine.' Delphine said, trying to sound calm. 'Just keep your arms tucked in by your side and get ready for the landing.' Delphine wasn't sure what good tucking her arms in would do her but she wanted to sound like she did it all the time.

Becky stepped into the portal, feet first, nothing happened at first but as she got in slightly further it was like she was sucked in. All of a sudden, she was surrounded by bright light and she was spinning, round and round. She wasn't sure how long she was spinning for but she knew she didn't like it. Just as she was beginning to panic, she landed in a dark cave, she thought she was back in the Blue John Cavern at first, but to her immense relief she saw Colby and Esme hugging and she knew they'd made it through okay.

Becky Bigteeth

A short while later, Sylvia came through the portal behind her and Delphine after that, they'd all made it through. They were all finally home. For Becky and Esme it was their first time back home where they truly belonged. It was dark in the caves here, it seemed even darker than back on earth and it was colder, a lot colder.

'Come on,' said Colby, 'we need to get moving before we all get hypothermia, it's bloody freezing.'

CHAPTER 23

Colby started to climb up the rocks, the others followed. It was pitch black. The only light available was from their headtorches and they threw off creepy looking shadows which unsettled Becky and Esme, the other three seemed undeterred.

Becky could hear weird scuttling noises coming from all around her, it sounded like huge furry creatures were surrounding them, running at one hundred miles an hour. She tried to put it out of her mind and focus on the climb. It was more tricky climbing here because the cold was starting to numb the ends of their fingers and the rocks were either slimy or icy, making it much harder to grab hold and pull themselves up.

Even more off putting than the noises were the constant shadows that Becky was convinced she could see out of the corner of her eye. She'd jerk her head quickly to the side, sure she was going to see something coming for her but every time there was nothing there. She'd get back to climbing and put it out of her mind for a few seconds but it wouldn't be long before another shadow played tricks on her.

Despite this, they managed to get through the hardest climb and the surface levelled out a bit before rising up again and leaving them one last, long ascent. Colby got up really quickly, he was much more adept at these conditions than the others and it showed, but he turned around to help the others often, meaning they all made pretty good time.

He leant down and held his arm out to lift Becky up. She took his arm but just as she looked up and got ready to boost herself up she saw a huge spider standing right behind Colby.

She screamed as loud as she could, the scream echoed through the caves for an age. Colby nearly fell off the edge of the rock he was on and the others all dropped to the floor, convinced they were under attack, their hearts beating two hundred times a minute.

'Becky, what is it?' Colby shouted once he'd regained his balance on the rock.

'Colby, look out, behind you.' Becky said, struggling to get her breathing back to normal, 'it's a spider, a massive spider!'

Colby seemed unconcerned and shrugged it off, 'oh that' he said, turning and looking behind him, 'that's not real, it's a cave painting, there's loads of them round here, it's nothing to worry about, Becky. Here, grab my hand.'

He held his arm out again, leaning over the edge. Becky grabbed it cautiously and boosted herself up. She wanted to sit on the floor and rest for thirty seconds while the others got up, but there was so much water dripping from the ceilings the floor was soaking, so she had to make do with leaning over to catch her breath.

The others were soon up with the help of Colby and he got moving straight away, 'come on' he said, 'look, there's light ahead, we're not far away now.'

Becky looked round for the cave painting of the spider she'd seen on the ledge but couldn't see it anywhere, 'Colby' she called to him, he turned around, still power walking his way out the cave. 'I couldn't see the painting of the spider on that ledge, did you say there were loads of them down here? I can't see any.'

Colby laughed, 'oh that, no, yeah, that was a real spider you saw. I lied about the paintings, the spiders in these caves are massive, but I knew you'd freak out if I told you back there. Come on, if you move fast they might leave us alone before we get out.'

Becky could feel panic taking over, she looked all around and above her to check she wasn't near any spiders. She wished she hadn't looked up, the ceiling was covered with bats, all hanging upside down asleep. Once the beam from her headtorch was on them it woke them up and sent them into a panic. They all started flying in different directions, there were thousands of them. They swooped down on the new arrivals, panicking them even more. Becky crouched down as low as she could while still moving forward, she'd slowed down and Esme bumped into the back of her.

In the confusion Becky wasn't sure what had bumped into her and became convinced it was a giant spider. She screamed again and ran, sprinting towards the daylight ahead, storming past Colby. He shouted for her to stop but she paid no attention and carried on running, she was almost out the cave. It was sunny outside, she knew she'd be safe once she got out and put her head down to run even faster, the weird bleating noises the bats were making spurring her on.

She was metres away from the cave entrance when suddenly Colby tackled her from behind, pushing them both outside into the sunshine. They landed on a cliff edge less than a metre wide with no railing to offer protection from falling. Becky landed face down looking over the edge of the ledge, the drop must have been five hundred metres, it was a straight drop down onto the rocks below.

Becky Bigteeth

Had Colby not tackled her she'd have run straight over the edge, he held her down for a few seconds while she regained her composure.

CHAPTER 24

Colby let Becky get up once he was happy she wasn't going to accidently throw herself over the edge. He sat down with his back to the wall, looking out over the amazing views. Becky was considerably less confident moving round on the cliff edge, she felt like she had to crawl along the floor, convinced that should any part of her body leave the ground she'd instantly be swept over the edge of the cliff.

She eventually managed to position herself so she was sat next to Colby. The heat was incredible, it reminded her of stepping off the plane at Lanzarote, the way it just hit you. She relaxed a lot once she was looking out over the magnificent landscape, she'd never seen anything like it, as amazing as the Peak District was, this place was on a whole new level.

Becky was so transfixed with looking at the view that she'd completely forgotten about the other three who were a considerable way back in the cave so when Delphine screeched 'you could have waited for us!' at the top of her voice as she came out the cave, Becky jumped out of her skin.

'Oh my god' she said, 'you three, I'm so sorry, I just completely freaked out. Colby said the giant spiders were real, then I saw all the bats and I totally lost it. I'm sorry.' Becky forced herself to stand up, but leant as tightly against the wall as she could.

Becky Bigteeth

'That's okay, Becs.' Said Esme, 'we're just glad you're safe. We tried to run after you but mum was struggling with the climb.'

They all looked over at Sylvia, she was in the cave entrance, bent double, furiously trying to get her breath back. She obviously needed a rest, they'd already had a very long day and they still had loads of ground to cover before getting some sleep.

'Come on' said Colby, slowly walking up the narrow winding path that circled round the mountain and seemed to lead right to the top. 'We're right near the summit here so we might as well go all the way to the top where there's more room and we can see the whole of The Kingdom. We'll have our lunch there and rest up a bit before heading down.'

He didn't wait for an answer or to see if any of the others were following him. Delphine motioned with her arms for the others to go and she'd follow on behind. Becky and Esme held hands as they walked in single file up the path, Esme went first, both of them stayed as close to the wall as they possibly could.

It took them ten minutes to get to the top, it would have taken them five if it wasn't for the overwhelming heat. They came to a clearing about ten metres across. Becky and Esme were still holding hands and they walked out into the centre, turning around to take in the whole view as they went.

They were completely mesmerised, as they looked down to one side they could see what looked like docklands, there were loads of ships being built. They could just make out hundreds of people helping to build them. They were climbing all over the ships, hammering them, raising masts and fixing flags to them. Beyond the boats they could see the sea, it stretched all the way to the horizon with no sign of any land nearby.

Becky and Esme turned round, taking in more of the sights. They looked over miles of desert. They couldn't see any people or animals but there were the odd patches of huge plants, they looked like cactus from here but they were so far away they couldn't be sure.

The desert eventually turned into more green land, Becky recognised it as the swamps that they'd seen through Janstel's eyes in the fire. The swamps led to the forests, and beyond that they could see Hightown Castle, it must have been hundreds of miles away from where they were but they could still see it quite clearly.

The more they looked, the more things struck them as odd. The sky above them was a weird light pink shade, there were no clouds anywhere near them but as they looked out towards the castle it seemed to get darker and darker. They could see rain coming down in the forests and the further out they looked the darker it became.

It was dark everywhere in the forest apart from where the castle was, oddly the castle seemed to have its very own climate because directly above the castle it seemed to be a nice sunny day, just like they were experiencing on top of the mountain.

'What's going on with the weather?' Esme asked as she continued to look out over The Kingdom.

'It will be that witch Velody no doubt.' Said Delphine, trying not to sound as angry as she felt. 'There was always talk that she was powerful enough to control the weather but most sensible elves and fairies ignored it, I mean, who or what could possibly be so powerful to be able to change the weather?' Delphine looked at Colby, the pair of them shared worried looks.

Becky Bigteeth

'What's happening with the ships?' Becky asked, 'it looks like they're building them in a hurry.'

'Who knows' said Colby, 'but your mother will have something to do with it, you can tell by the flags on the ships.' He looked out at the ships a bit longer before saying anything, 'she must be planning something, I can't imagine it's anything good.'

CHAPTER 25

The group got their food out and sat down on the clearing to have a picnic. For the first few minutes they said nothing, just ate their food and took in the new surroundings. When they were nearly done eating, they started to get their energy back so talked more about Elfaron and the history of The Kingdom.

'There's been elves and fairies on Elfaron for generations.' Said Sylvia, 'no-one knows when we arrived or if we ever lived elsewhere, it seems that we've always lived here, but the trolls? The trolls are fairly new. They first arrived about fifty years ago. Legend has it that Handor, the troll king had seduced Santure, the queen of the sea.

'Santure was so in love with Handor that she granted him his wish of having safe passage from Troll Island to Elfaron. It's a journey thousands had tried before but none had made it. The Santurn sea is so treacherous no ships survive the journey, but Santure made it safe for Handor and ten of his best troll soldiers, six men, four women. Unbeknownst to Santure though, Handor already had a wife and young son, he had seduced the queen of the sea so his family could set up home in Elfaron. He'd grown tired of Troll Island and wanted an adventure.

'When they first arrived the elves and fairies were very worried, they panicked that the trolls were here to take over and attack them and take their homes. But Handor and his small army caused no trouble, they asked for a small piece of land in the Swamplands, far away from Hightown Castle and before too long the panic died down and the trolls were all but forgotten about. They settled in the Swamplands, had children and slowly increased in number.

'Handor passed away about thirty years ago and his son, Crowton, became the new king. Whilst Handor was happy living a quiet life with his people in The Swamplands, Crowton had more ambition. He dreamed of living somewhere more pleasant than the swamps and convinced most of the army, now a couple of hundred trolls, to pack up and move to the Woodlands where it was drier and food was easier to come by.

'It didn't seem to be a problem at first but pretty soon the trolls started to steal animals from our farms and even rob people on their way to the castle. At first the Elf King, Wantrow, your Grandfather.' Sylvia continued, nodding to Becky, 'ignored the small crimes, but the trolls got braver and more dangerous by the day until one day they even attacked the queen when she was out for a ride on her horse.

'Wantrow was outraged. He rode out to confront Crowton and banished him and his people from The Kingdom entirely. He had the huge watch tower extended at Hightown Castle and made into a dome so he could see the whole of The Kingdom and keep an eye out for any trolls trying to get back in The Kingdom.'

Sylvia stopped her story for a minute so she could finish off her cheese sandwiches, their food had attracted a big blue bird, it was bigger than any bird Becky had ever seen in Castleton, bigger than an eagle and totally unfazed by their presence. At first it circled the group, then, when it saw that some food was being dropped it landed on the mountaintop and slowly walked towards them, hoping for some handouts. Although the bird looked friendly, Becky and Esme were wary of the size of its bright yellow beak. Delphine slowly stood up and walked towards the bird with some bread in her hands.

'Here, sweetie, that's a good boy' she said, softly whistling to greet him, 'don't be scared' she said to Becky and Esme. 'This handsome chap is called a Beachy bird, they're really friendly once they get to know you. If we give him some food now he might stick with us for a while and who knows, he could even help us out. Beachy birds are very good at finding food and water.'

Becky and Esme stood up and slowly walked towards the Beachy bird. He jumped back a bit until deciding that they were genuine offers of food and then he jumped forward, and gently took the bread Becky was holding in her hands. He gulped all that down then devoured the pork pie crust that Esme was holding. He didn't take any time to chew it, just swallowed it whole. He flew up in the air, revealing magnificent yellow feathers on the underside of his wings, then landed on Becky's shoulder and nuzzled her face, making her laugh out in surprise.

'Hey, he likes you!' said Colby, standing up to make a fuss of the Beachy bird.

'How do you know it's a boy?' Esme asked, stroking his back.

'Because he has blue feathers, the females have red and green feathers and are quite a lot smaller.' Said Colby, 'now that he trusts you he'll be your friend for life, he might not be with you forever, they like to be on their own a lot, but he'll always be watching out for you.'

Becky Bigteeth

Becky was amazed, she'd always wanted a pet. Hatty used to have a hamster called Hunter when she was younger and they both loved to play with him. Becky would often ask Aunt Sylvia if she could have one too but she said they didn't belong in cages and should be in the wild.

'What are you going to call him?' Esme asked Becky.

'Hhhmmm,' Becky thought for a second, 'I'm going to call him Frankie.'

'That suits him' said Aunt Sylvia, 'you look like a Frankie, don't you, boy?' She rubbed his chin with her fingers whilst making cooing noises. Frankie looked at her blankly then jumped up and started circling the top of the mountain again.

'Come on' said Colby, 'it looks like he wants us to go with him, we've had a long enough rest, let's get going. The Wastelands go on for ages and I don't want to spend more than one night out there.' He nodded towards the vast desert that sat between them and The Swamplands, it was almost as if Frankie knew where they were headed. He set off flying down the side of the mountain, occasionally turning back to see if they were following.

Dan Watford

CHAPTER 26

It took a while for the group to get going, they had all been pretty cosy on top of the mountain and their shoulders were already sore from the rucksacks, so it was painful and inconvenient to put them back on. Becky and Esme in particular needed quite a bit of cajoling from Delphine to hurry up.

The path down the mountain was steep and narrow and had a lot of loose rocks which meant they had to be extra careful with each step so as not to stumble over the edge of the mountain. Becky and Esme held hands all the way down with Esme leading the way and pointing out lizards and spiders that were running and jumping over the rocks slightly in front of them, Becky didn't look once, she just feigned interest so as not to offend her cousin. In reality she would rather not have known how many animals were in such close proximity. She knew lizards were pretty harmless on earth, but on this foreign planet, who knew? They could be poisonous, or even worse, man-eating lizards that could magically grow ten foot high and bite their heads off. She doubted this were true but it didn't stop her from fearing the worst and walking a lot of the way down with her eyes screwed as tightly as she dared without actually closing them.

Becky's worst fears were not realised however, and the lizards left them well enough alone to allow for them to reach the bottom of the mountain unscathed. Once they made it to the bottom, they just had to negotiate their way over some sharp, jagged boulders before they gave way to the stony and sandy wilderness that was The Wastelands.

The five of them squinted and looked off into the distance. The Swamplands seemed to be a million miles away from where they were. The wind was howling and blowing sand directly into their faces, it seemed determined to keep them pinned to the side of the mountain.

'Hey, guys, wait!' Delphine suddenly shouted, 'can you believe that in all the excitement I've forgotten the most important part of our journey?'

'What's that?' Esme asked.

'The transformation of course. You don't expect to stay looking like that now we're on Elfaron do you? People would think we're aliens. Come on, everyone in a circle, holding hands.' The group did as they were told, all five of them stood in a circle facing each other. 'Now close your eyes and relax.' Said Delphine. Then she started mumbling something in a foreign language, quietly at first, then building up louder and louder until she was staring up at the sky, shouting at the top of her voice.

Becky held Esme's and Colby's hands as tightly as she could. The wind got stronger and stronger until the sand hitting her face started to become really painful. Suddenly her whole body was in agony, her back felt like it was going to rip into two, she felt for sure that her head was caving in on itself and her legs seemed like they were being pulled out of their sockets. The pain became so bad that she let go of Colby and Esme's hands to grab her stomach, she doubled over on the ground, she wasn't sure if the screaming she could hear was Delphine's or her own.

Dan Watford

The stretching and splitting and crushing all over her body got worse and worse until she thought she was going to pass out, but then it was over. Just like that the pain had gone away and all she could feel was relief, she opened her eyes, the wind had stopped and the sand that had been flying around had now settled on the floor. The sky was still a beautiful pink colour but she could see planets and moons as well now. She looked round, suddenly she could see The Swamplands much more clearly and she could have sworn she could see people walking around even though they were still miles away. When she looked at the others, she couldn't believe it.

She saw Delphine first, the beautiful, dark skinned dance teacher she knew from earth still looked similar but she seemed to have shrunk about a foot, grown her hair another foot or so and her skin was now a magnificent leafy green colour. Standing proudly from her back were two enormous wings. All the stories Becky had read about fairies had said that fairy wings were light, delicate things, but Delphine's wings were strong looking, heavy duty wings, they looked like more an extension of her body than an addition to her body. Becky stared, slack jawed at her and walked right up to her, examining every inch of her body.

'What are you staring at?' Delphine asked, smiling. 'Haven't you ever seen a fairy before?'

Becky smiled and shook her head, 'Delphine, my God, you look incredible!' Becky reached out to touch Delphine's wings, 'these are amazing!' she said.

'What do mine look like Becs?' Esme asked.

Becky spun round, she had been so mesmerised with Delphine that she had even forgotten the others were there. She looked at her cousin, who was now a much lighter green than Delphine. She'd

94

also shrunk a bit, but her arms were really well defined and her wings were also very impressive. Whilst Esme's skin was a fairly light green her wings contrasted and were a much darker colour, almost brown, but hers too looked like very strong wings indeed.

'Oh my God, mum, look at you.' Said Esme, staring in disbelief at her mum, Becky looked as well and the difference was so vast, she barely even recognised her aunty. Her greying hair had turned back to a bright yellow, not blonde, but yellow. Her wrinkles had all but disappeared and her stature was so much more confident, she was stood up almost straight as opposed to the half-bent crookedness she had on earth. There was one obvious difference between Sylvia and Esme, Sylvia no longer had her wings, there was still a noticeable bump on her back where her wings had been but Sylvia seemed so unbothered by it that it was difficult to think much of it.

Becky walked up to her aunty to touch her face, 'hey' said Sylvia, backing away whilst smiling.

'Sorry aunty' said Becky, 'it's just that you look so good, I can't believe it, you look thirty years younger!'

'What about me?' Asked Colby, they all looked over at him, he was also a bit smaller but hadn't shrunk that much so was taller than the others. His hair had grown in length, shooting straight upwards out of his head, making him seem taller than he was. His skin was also a light green, similar to Esme's, and he seemed to have gained a fair amount of muscle mass, he reminded Becky of the athletes at the Olympics. She couldn't see an ounce of fat on him and although he was still his usual smiley self, he now seemed a lot more determined and focused as well. Becky wasn't sure how she could tell the difference, but his eyes, which were a magical emerald green colour, seemed to glow with an intensity that he didn't have back on earth.

Becky looked down at her own hands, they too were green, lighter than Delphine's but darker than the others. She looked up at her arms and was impressed with how strong they looked, then she got a glimpse of her own wings over her shoulder. They were big, the top of the wings came well over the top of her shoulders, the tip of the wings pointed up towards the sky. She tried to flap them, unsure of how or what to do but nothing happened, she focused with all her might but still nothing happened.

'I can't move my wings.' She said to the others, a trifle concerned.

'Oh, don't worry, Becky.' Said Delphine, 'it will take you a while to learn the skills, don't worry, we'll all teach you both.' And with that, Delphine jumped high into the air, she spread her wings out and tensed them, she almost stayed exactly where she was in mid-air, dropping at such a slow rate she was like a feather falling slowly to the ground. Then with one big flap of her wings, Delphine was suddenly twenty feet in the air. She flew higher and higher, then back and forth, howling and screaming with joy as she flew. After a minute or so she landed. 'Wow, after all this time, that felt really good!' She said.

Colby then started running and jumping, away from the others then back towards them. After a couple of quick runs back and forth, faster than Usain Bolt, he started to do somersaults, spinning himself round faster and faster, and bouncing higher and higher. Becky and Esme looked at each other, each bewildered at what Colby and Delphine were achieving. Becky couldn't wait to start training if it meant she'd end up flying like Delphine or running like Colby, they both seemed superhuman.

Becky Bigteeth

'Come on' said Colby once he'd finished his running, 'there's no more time to lose, we want to be well on our way by nightfall. By the looks of it, there's never a guarantee the sun will rise again here so we'd best make the most of it. Delphine, are you staying with us or flying ahead?'

'I'll stay with you guys, at least for a bit, help you get settled in.' She smiled at Becky and Esme, 'but I warn you, if you start moaning or boring me, I'm out of here.' She winked at the pair of them. The five of them walked in a line, all chatting and laughing, excited for the journey, as Frankie flew overhead, staying just a few metres in front of them so he could keep an eye out for any potential danger that might befall his new found master.

CHAPTER 27

The sun was unrelenting all afternoon. The group got through most of their water supplies in the first couple of hours. Colby had to warn them all to slow down as there was no water for miles in any direction in The Wastelands, and The Swamplands seemed to be getting no closer. Delphine offered to fly ahead and bring some water back, but Colby was worried she'd put too much strain on her wings and could end up in the middle of nowhere so told her they needed to stick together. Delphine whispered something under her breath than none of the others could hear, but it didn't sound very flattering towards Colby, then she flew ahead for a bit before coming back with an excited look on her face.

'Colby!' she shouted, pointing into the distance, the others all looked, their eyesight was much improved since they'd transformed and they could all see the group of plants she was pointing at. They were huge cactus plants, there must have been about twenty plants altogether. The ones on the outside were small, they got bigger and bigger closer to the centre, leading to a huge one in the middle. 'It's Mordren fruit, Colby, we haven't had any for years, I'm going to bring some back for us.'

'No' said Colby before Delphine had a chance to fly away again, 'you know how good I am at fetching Mordren fruit, let me. After all, they say you never lose your touch. Watch this.' And with that, he sprinted towards the Mordren fruit plants. He was there in no time. The others jogged behind, taking a lot longer than he did to get close. Colby was standing statue still with his knife out, planning his course of action. Delphine ushered the others to stop well behind him to give him room to work.

'This should be funny' she whispered to the other three, 'I've been telling him for years now that he's not doing enough training and he'll be unfit when we get home but her wouldn't listen. Sure he looks fast to you guys, but trust me, he should be running at twice the speed he is now. He's in for a shock here, just you watch.' Delphine smiled at the others and they all sat down to watch Colby bring back some fruit.

Once he'd planned his route, Colby slowly took a couple of steps forwards, then burst into a run. He started running towards one of the smaller plants on the outside before turning towards a bigger one at the last second. The others watched in amazement as the plant that he'd been running for suddenly started moving, it seemed to be moving away from him before letting out a high-pitched wail that got louder and louder.

Colby stopped dead in his tracks a couple of metres away from the plants. He stood looking utterly defeated as the small plant's wailing seemed to wake up the other plants and they all started wailing too. Then one of the bigger plants that he'd been running towards suddenly swiped one of its branches out at Colby, almost slamming it straight into his arm. Colby noticed at the very last second and managed to jump out of the way. The plants all looked like people rather than plants now, they all seemed to be waving their spiky arms at him as if trying to stick him with their prickles and they were all wailing so loud it sounded like it might wake the dead.

Colby turned back to the others and walked towards them with his head down and his shoulders slumped, he looked utterly embarrassed. Delphine suddenly burst into a screeching laughter, throwing her head back as if she'd just been told the funniest joke ever. The others couldn't help but join in laughing and soon they were all in stitches.

'Sorry, Colby,' said Sylvia as Colby got back to them, 'we're not laughing at you.'

'Yes, we are.' Delphine said, in between fits of laughter, 'we definitely are!'

CHAPTER 28

I t took several hours for Colby to get over his embarrassment of the Mordren fruit, it was almost dark before he even spoke to the others again.

'Right' he said, 'this seems as good a place as any to try and get some sleep, we've all had a long day and I think we've learned quite enough about The Wastelands for one day. Delphine, are you going to fetch Blaze so we can get out of here?' He asked.

'You betcha' Delphine said in the fake London accent she was so keen on using. 'I'll see you lot soon.' She smiled at Becky and Esme, 'you all stay together, you understand? There's a lot of danger out here, you might not be able to see it but rest assured, it's out there.'

'Like what?' Becky asked, not really wanting to know.

'All sorts,' said Delphine, 'but the worst are the Dagger Spiders and the Red Wolves. Dagger Spiders have razor sharp legs which they use as a weapon to take down their prey, they're only small but they can do a lot of damage to elves and fairies. The Red Wolves hunt in packs, they sleep in the caves in the daytime and come out at night to hunt. They like to have fun with their prey and make sure they know they're being hunted, they'll howl and snarl and scream to scare their prey and pounce when they're too petrified to move.'

'Wait' said Esme, 'when you say they sleep in the caves, do you mean the caves we arrived in?'

'Never mind that,' said Colby waving the question away, 'You go Delphine, we'll get some sleep and see you and Blaze back here, quick as you can.'

And with that, Delphine flapped her wings and was up in the air heading towards The Swamplands. The others watched as she went, then got their sleeping bags out and lay down on the ground.

Becky didn't think she'd be able to sleep on the hard ground, but within minutes she was fast asleep. She dreamt about her mother again, she dreamt she was lying on the ground looking up at Frankie flying in the sky, when suddenly three black crows swarmed around Frankie and started flying with him until he flew away. Then the crows stared circling where Becky was lying, she wanted to get up and run, but for some reason she was frozen to the ground. She tried to scream but nothing came out. The crows were getting closer and closer until she could make out their faces.

One had the haggard old face of Velody, another, the strong and determined face of Aldeese, and the last had the beautiful, smiling face of her mother. Then the birds landed on the ground right near her.

Becky's whole body tensed up as the birds got closer and closer, the one that looked like Aldeese started pecking on her leg, while the one that looked like Velody started pecking on her belly. The crow that looked like Gelda stood near Becky's face and started talking.

'Look at your beautiful face, my darling daughter' said Gelda. 'Look at your sleek hair, your strong cheekbones, and your teeth. My goodness, they are amazing.' Becky flinched as the crow pecked at the ground right next to her head. 'And of course, your eyes.' Said the crow, 'who could forget your eyes? They look so tasty, in fact, I think I'll try one.'

Becky screamed as the crow's head hovered over hers, Gelda stuck her tongue out as if she was licking her lips and went to peck Becky's right eye. Becky screamed, very loudly. She managed to close her eyes when she felt something shaking her violently.

'Becky! Becky!' she heard, it was Colby, shouting right in her face. 'It's okay, Becky, you were having a nightmare, you're safe now, it's okay.'

Becky sat up, still shaking, not knowing where she was. She managed to slow her breathing down a bit and sat up. The others were all awake now, she started telling them all about her nightmare when she was interrupted by a deadly sounding howling coming from far off in the distance.

Colby swore and started shoving things in his rucksack. 'It's Red Wolves' he said, 'the screaming must have woken them up. Come on, we need to move, now!'

CHAPTER 29

The four of them frantically forced everything into their rucksacks and threw them on their shoulders before sprinting away from the howling. Fortunately, the howling was coming from the caves, so it meant Becky and her friends were running towards The Swamplands. Unfortunately, every time the wolves howled, they seemed to be much closer than they were before.

Esme, Becky and Colby were decent runners, all in good shape and all pumped up with enough fear and adrenaline to ensure they didn't slow down. That was until they looked round and saw how far behind Aunt Sylvia was. She was desperately making herself go as fast as she could but she was panicking and her desperation was causing her to overexert herself and she kept losing her balance.

Becky and Esme ran back to help her, but Colby passed them with ease and pointed for them to keep heading towards the Swamplands. 'Go' he shouted as he neared Aunt Sylvia, 'there's no need for all of us to get behind, you two go as fast as you can, I'll make sure she's okay, I promise.'

Becky ignored Colby's orders and kept running back to help, but Esme grabbed her by the arm and pulled her back. 'No, he's right, Becky.' Esme said, 'there's no point all of us going back, she'll be fine, Colby will make sure of it.' Becky looked at her cousin in horror, was she really suggesting they leave Aunt Sylvia behind? Esme's own mother? Becky was shocked, she looked back again and saw that Colby had Aunt Sylvia on his back and was catching them up, that was enough reassurance for Becky and she ran, following Esme.

Rather than lag behind because of the weight, Colby actually managed to catch the two girls up so all four of them were together again. He ran on ahead for a few more metres before stopping, putting Aunt Sylvia gently on the ground and reaching for his bow and arrow. He could see the menacing green eyes of the wolves lighting up the horizon. The bright eyes gave him an easy target, although they were moving very fast.

He quickly fired on arrow at a pair of eyes without success. He fired another two in the same direction but still had no joy. Then he took his time on the fourth arrow, and braced himself on the ground, firmly fixing his gaze right between a pair of shining eyes. This arrow found it's mark, they heard a thud, followed by a whimper, which soon changed into a howl of pain, before the sound died out altogether, he'd taken one out but there was still loads left, he decided to make another run for it.

The wolves were just metres away from the group now, and The Swamplands still seemed to be miles away. They ran past a dark patch of plants, Colby shoved Aunt Sylvia towards the plants, then Esme, 'come on' he said to Becky, pointing towards the plants. 'These Mordren Fruit will give us protection but don't make any noise.'

They knelt together at the bottom of a large Mordren plant. Colby put his fingers to his lips. The Mordren fruit were almost blind, relying mainly on sound to root out their enemies. If the four of them stayed calm there was a chance they'd be able to hide in the fruit and wait for the red wolves to get fed up and look for different prey.

Becky, Esme and Sylvia huddled together beneath a huge branch of the Mordren fruit. Even though it was dark now, Becky could see the thorns on the arm glistening in the moonlight, she shuddered to think of the damage one of those could do. The wolves had gone quiet whilst they circled the Mordren fruit, looking for a way in, they didn't get too close, all the animals in the Wastelands knew how dangerous the Mordren fruit were.

Colby had his bow and arrow loaded and held it facing the wolves as they moved in closer, looking for a gap in the fruit. Becky was so focused on where the wolves were that she didn't notice a spider, five inches in diameter, slowly lowering itself onto her shoulder from the Mordren fruit above.

The spider landed so gently on Becky's shoulder that she didn't notice at first, when it started walking down her arm, she thought it was Sylvia or Esme stroking her for comfort. She looked down expecting to be comforted, it took a second for her eyes to adjust enough to see what was actually on her arm, when the penny dropped, she jerked suddenly, throwing the hairy creature off as quickly as she could before screaming.

The spider splatted onto a thorn on the Mordren fruit, which immediately starting throwing its arms around, frantically trying to maim someone, anyone, it didn't matter who. Within seconds the entire orchard of Mordren fruit was awake and screeching and waving their thorny arms around. The wolves were startled and moved back to safety but didn't run off entirely, they wanted to see what would happen to their dinner.

Becky Bigteeth

Colby fired three arrows as quickly as he could at the large Mordren fruit they had been sheltering under, this bought them enough time to hurry out into the open. Aunt Sylvia tripped in her hurry to get away, she twisted her ankle and just as she was getting up, the Mordren fruit swiped with its huge, thorny arm and scraped the huge needles all down Sylvia's back as it passed. Sylvia screamed in agony and lurched forward a bit further, desperate to get out of range of a second swipe. The arm came back her way just as she was getting up and things looked hopeless. Right before she was stabbed, Colby dived at her, spearing her midsection with his shoulder with enough force to send her soaring four foot into the air. The pair of them landed on the floor, Colby on top of the already injured Sylvia, who was now winded and had blood pouring out of her back.

Becky and Esme grabbed them both by the arms and pulled them along the floor as fast as they could, out of reach of the Mordren fruit. Just as they felt they were clear and safe, they heard a menacing growl behind them, the wolves had moved in again. This time, they'd sent the youngest and fastest wolf to do some damage. Colby, Becky and Esme, stood over Sylvia on the ground and tried to form a strong pack. The young wolf seemed undeterred and prepared to pounce, it ran towards them with its teeth bared, just as it left the ground something flew from the sky and started pecking the wolf in the eyes. The wolf howled in agony, shaking his head wildly before retreating back to the pack.

They had been saved, at least in the short term, by their new friend, Frankie. Becky burst out laughing in relief as Frankie circled overhead, threatening any other wolves that wanted to charge, none did for the time being. Instead, they spread out forming a wide semi-circle around their prey, forcing them back towards the Mordren fruit.

The four of them had run out of ideas and were just contemplating which would be the best way to go, eaten by wolves or carved up by Mordren fruit, when they heard something above them. Delphine had made it back with Blaze, the wolves watched helplessly as the flying horse landed, and Delphine helped her friends onto his back. In no time at all they were airborne and flying far away from danger, far away from The Wastelands. They headed towards The Swamplands.

CHAPTER 30

Becky held onto Blaze for dear life as they flew faster and faster away from the danger. She could hear the red wolves below howling in anger that their dinner had been taken away from them. She looked out over the top of Blaze's right wing, it was very dark so she couldn't see much below but the sights above her head were glorious.

She could see hundreds of shooting stars flying in all directions, there seemed to be millions of normal stars too, some tiny, some impressively big. What caught Becky's eye the most was the moon, at least, she thought it was the moon. It was much bigger than the moon on earth and gave off a faint green glow.

Becky was struck at how quickly the darkness had fallen on them, it seemed like one minute they were baking in the heat of The Wastelands, the next they were running away from the red wolves in darkness. She was really cold as well, but she thought that might be because of how high up they were flying. Becky looked down again, hundreds of camp fires dotted the landscape ahead, some seemed close, others seemed to be miles and miles away.

Esme grabbed Becky's arm as they felt Blaze descending, the two cousins looked at each other, both smiling, very excited but also wary about what lay ahead. Sylvia and Colby were on Blaze's left wing and both were having a good natter, Becky couldn't hear what they were talking about but she knew they'd both be so excited to finally be home. They'd been away since Becky was a baby, not seeing any of their friends or family and never being able to visit home, all to help keep Becky alive, she couldn't believe the sacrifices they'd made for her.

The closer Blaze got to the ground, the faster he seemed to go, all the while Delphine was singing his praises and howling with delight at finally being reunited with her pet. When they landed on the ground, Colby jumped off Blaze like a gymnast, pushing himself off with his hands, he spun round in mid-air before landing firmly on his feet. He'd barely been on the ground a second before he got rugby tackled by someone screaming his name and hugging all the air out of him.

Sylvia dismounted much more gingerly than Colby, but again, as soon as she was on the ground, she was swamped with people welcoming her home. Becky and Esme stayed where they were for a second while they watched the others. Colby was still being hugged by the lady who kept kissing him on the cheeks and screaming with delight.

Delphine climbed down from her saddle on the middle of Blaze's back and stood in front of the girls, holding her hand down to help them climb down. 'Come on, you two.' She said, beaming her usual smile from ear to ear. 'Don't look so nervous, this is your home, these people are your friends, they've all been dying to meet you both, let's go and have a drink.'

Esme jumped down first and turned to help Becky get down. As Becky climbed down, everyone gathered round, staring at her as if she was a waxwork. She was uncomfortable at being the centre of attention, she didn't know where to look or what to say. There were two men, one slim with long blond hair that looked like it hadn't been brushed in weeks, and the other was fairly short, well-built with blue hair slicked right back, it looked like it was dripping with oil.

The woman had stopped kissing Colby long enough to join the crowd as well, although she stood next to him with her arm round him. She had plaited her dark hair into three plaits, two on her right-hand side and one big plait on the left-hand side which she threw over her shoulder. She smiled at Becky as if they'd known each other a lifetime before walking up to her and holding out her hand. Becky noticed how strong the woman's arms looked and how much bigger her wings were than the others, but what struck her the most was how instantly drawn to her she was, she was mesmerized as the lady started talking.

'Becky, I'm Tendril, it's so nice to finally meet you.' She said, Becky noticed a slight twang in her voice, she wondered if they all spoke like that, she hoped so, it was the best accent she'd ever heard. It reminded her of the way they used to speak on Neighbours, her and Esme used to love that show. 'You've done so well putting up with these two for so long, how have you managed it?' Tendril asked pointing towards Colby and Delphine with a smirk on her face. Tendril's green eyes reminded Becky of a necklace she used to have when she was young. They were so green, they didn't look real, yet on Tendril they seemed perfectly natural.

'And you' Tendril said, throwing her arm round Esme's shoulder, 'you must be the famous Esme we've all heard so much about. What a job you've done keeping all these four in check, no wonder your mum's so proud of you!'

Esme couldn't conceal her pride and delight at being so openly praised. She too liked Tendril straightaway and both girls liked her even more when she called Colby a loonpanter, neither of them had any idea what a loonpanter was but they both knew it was an insult and they both thought it was hilarious.

Their laughter quickly stopped and they both grabbed each other's hands tightly as they watched a huge ogre like creature come stomping around the corner. His walk looked uncomfortable as his huge legs seemed to rub against each other and his arms were so big he struggled to relax them. His huge forehead and bushy eyebrows made it look like he was constantly angry, he walked over to Becky and Esme and they both cowered away, both girls wondering why no-one was saving them from this furious monster.

Suddenly, the giant dropped to one knee and bowed his head at them, 'Your Majesty,' he said in a manner so timid it seemed comical coming from someone his size, 'this is indeed an honour, thank you for coming to save us Your Majesty.' The giant again bowed his head.

'What. On. Earth. Are. You. Doing. You. Dufus?' Tendril said, pausing for effect after each word. 'Lower the drawbridge, Ergo, how on earth are you ever going to get them to fight for us if they think we're all a bunch of grass nibblers going around bowing and kneeling in front of people.'

'Oh my god.' Said Becky, surprising herself at talking aloud, 'you're Ergo, you're the leader, we've heard all about you, haven't we, Esme?' Esme smiled and nodded, she was too relieved that he wasn't going to eat them to say anything.

'You've heard of me?' Ergo asked, clearly delighted at his new found fame.

'Of course they've heard of you, Ergo.' Said Colby walking up to him and reaching up to put a hand on his old friend's shoulder. 'We couldn't possibly tell them about The Kingdom without telling them all about the Ergo Six Crew, could we?' Ergo smiled from ear to ear, the Princess knew who he was? He almost pinched himself to make sure it was real, it turned out he wouldn't have to pinch himself, Tendril did it for him before standing between him and Colby.

'That's right, girls' she said, 'we're the Ergo Six Crew, the most fearsome gang in all of The Kingdom. Heroes of the people. Champions of the underdogs.' All six of them stood proudly in a line, their heads held high and their chests pumped up, the Crew was reunited and they were ready to take back what was rightfully theirs.

CHAPTER 31

The group all sat down round the campfire. Becky and Esme sat close together and while the others were all busy catching up and getting drunk, the girls had time to take in the scenery. The lush green of the trees surrounding them was a stark contrast to the harsh yellow of The Wastelands. They could hear jungle noises all around them, monkeys screeching, birds singing and insects in the background clicking and whirring around.

They were sat on small seats made out of wood and some kind of leaf strung between the wood offering them a fair amount of comfort whilst also keeping them off the damp ground. Although they were about twenty metres away from the nearest swamp, the ground near them was so soggy it felt like quicksand. The seats were all fastened to a large plank to stop them from sinking into the ground. Becky wondered how long living in an environment like this would be sustainable, although the cabins around them were all on props high above the wet ground. Surely it was only a matter of time before the damp crept up the wood and started to rot them?

Just then, Becky felt something sharp dig into her shoulder, she flinched and looked round, relieved and delighted to see that it was Frankie. 'Oh, Frankie! You've found me, you clever boy.' She said, hugging him as tightly as she dared. The others stopped talking and all came around to admire Becky's new pet. They all agreed he was a fine-looking Beachy bird, Tendril even said he would be a fine addition to their army.

'Our army?' Becky asked, shocked that they would have enough troops to be considered an army.

'Oh yeah' said Tendril casually, 'we've been busy while you lot have been sunning yourselves on a foreign planet, we've been recruiting as many elves and fairies as we could, we've got loads willing to fight for their real queen.' Tendril nodded to Becky.

'That's great, Tendy.' Said Colby, 'how many have you recruited? Let's see, there's probably fifty thousand elves and fairies in The Kingdom, nearly all will be brave warriors, all wanting to see the real prophecy on the throne to lead them to greatness. How many do we have? Thirty thousand?'

Colby and Delphine stood together, excited to hear, the others shifted around and looked at each other sheepishly, 'erm, two thousand.' Said Tendril, looking for the first time anything other than amazingly confident, 'and I've told you before, Colby, don't call me Tendy.'

'Two thousand?' Said Delphine, 'what have you been doing all these years? I could have raised two thousand using smoke signals from earth!'

'You don't understand, Delphine' Tendril said, 'things are different these days, people are scared, and with good reason. Gelda's powerful, she might not be the true prophecy and she might have faked a lot of her credentials, but she's amassed a powerful troll army, pretty much without anyone really noticing. There just seems to be more and more of them coming in, they've taken over the castle and are now moving into The Woodlands, it won't be long before we're all driven out to The Wastelands.'

Martinez stood up, 'we won't let that happen, Tendril, I promise.' He said, putting an arm round her. 'But what she's saying is right. And it's not just the trolls that are a danger, that witch she's got working for her, Velody, she's a dangerous woman. Look how dark it is,' he said, waving his arms at the sky to drive his point home, 'you would think its midnight it's so dark. It isn't, it's half past seven and it's been dark for hours, the days are getting shorter and shorter. The sun rises at ten and sets at four, and it gets worse the closer you get to the castle.'

Becky thought back to when they were on top of the mountain looking out over The Kingdom, it had looked much darker towards the castle, at the time, she thought it must have been because it was so far away but now what Martinez was saying made sense.

'Why would they do that though?' asked Esme.

'Because Gelda wants everyone to be afraid of her and to be fearful of rebellion. In her eyes people are more scared in the dark, so the longer they're in the dark for, the longer they're afraid.'

They all looked into the fire contemplating their situation before Colby clapped his hands together and suggested they go inside to sort out sleeping arrangements and have a few more drinks.

CHAPTER 32

They were all staying in the same cabin, it was handmade out of a strong dark wood, wide stairs led up to a big front door. As Becky walked through the front door, she noticed large clumps knocked out of the top of the doorway and wondered how that could have happened. Her question was soon answered as she heard Ergo bang his head on the way in, she looked round to see him rubbing his head and cursing under his breath.

The cabin looked fairly small from the outside but once they were inside it seemed much more spacious. There was an enclosed fire in the middle of the room with a chimney going straight up through the roof, the fire was kicking off an enormous amount of heat, it felt like a sauna.

There were beds all along the far end from where Becky stood, some were raised off the ground, others were just mattresses on the floor. Becky was stood next to a large dining table, the whole of the table top was covered with a map. She could see different colours and regions on but couldn't read the writing, she guessed it was a map of The Kingdom though. Frankie flew off her shoulder and landed on the map, pecking at a piece of green fruit that had been left on the table, it was about the size of a small melon but looked soft and fleshy all around the outside.

Esme had left her side and was sitting on one of the beds with Delphine, the pair of them looked to be in deep discussion.

Becky couldn't tell what they were talking about but they kept glancing over at her and looking away whenever she caught their eye. Ergo put his hand on her shoulder, she jumped slightly and he looked mortified to have scared her.

'Oh, Your Majesty, I'm so sorry to have scared you.' He said, bowing his head in shame, 'I didn't mean to, I just wanted to offer you a drink.'

'That's fine, you didn't scare me' Becky said, trying to calm him down, 'I was just deep in thought, that's all. Thanks, I will have a drink.' She took the wooden beer tankard off him and took a sip of the brown, frothy drink inside. She winced so hard at the sourness of the drink that her lips pulled back over her teeth. She creased her eyes shut as well, unable to open them until her taste buds went back to normal. 'Blimey, what's in that?' She asked, her eyes still closed. When she opened them, she jumped again, Ergo was right in her face, examining her teeth as closely as he could.

'Oh my, Your Majesty, I'm so sorry, I've scared you again.' Ergo was very flustered now and didn't know where to look, he thought about walking off, but where would he go? 'I meant no offense, I'm sorry. It's just I'd heard so much about your giant teeth and I didn't believe it, I couldn't believe that anyone could have teeth like yours.' Becky was hoping he wasn't intentionally insulting her. 'But now I've seen them for myself, all I can say is, wow. They're incredible. Part of me always doubted you were the true prophecy, but not anymore.' He bowed his head again before taking a long sip of his beer.

The others all gathered round, trying to get a glimpse of her teeth without actually daring to ask. Colby broke up the awkward silence, 'let's have a toast' he said with his quiet but firm voice, 'to friends, old and new.'

'To friends, old and new.' They all repeated, Colby held his drink out in the middle of the group, Delphine joined him and held hers next to his, Ergo did the same, then Sylvia, then Martinez. Becky was last to hold hers out, not because she didn't want to but because she'd been too busy staring at her new friends. They were all so different, each with their own unique features but they all shared the same determined look, masked under calm faces, all except Martinez, who just looked angry, very angry. As Becky held her drink out, they all banged them together fiercely, sending drink flying high up in the air, some nearly landed on Frankie but he squawked and managed to move out the way, just in time.

Becky and Esme watched as all the others downed their drinks in seconds, Sylvia included, the pair were gobsmacked. They tried their best to keep up but could only manage a couple of sips at a time. 'Don't worry, you two' said Delphine after watching them struggle for a while, 'it's an acquired taste but you'll get used to it. I'm going to get some food, who else wants some?' To Delphine's disgust everyone said they wanted something, 'I was only being polite, I didn't think anyone would actually want anything, come on, Esme, you can help me with the burgers.' Esme smirked at Becky then followed Delphine outside, she daren't disobey her.

'Sit down, Becky, you must be exhausted.' Said Stanton.

'Thanks' said Becky before sitting down next to Tendril, she looked back at Stanton and noticed how unwarrior-like he looked. The others all looked like they could handle themselves in a fight, but Stanton looked more like an office clerk in fancy dress than a real warrior. Before she could ponder that more, she was distracted by Tendril stroking her wings.

'Sorry, Becky.' Tendril said, although she didn't actually stop stroking her wings even if she was sorry, 'I was just checking how strong they were, I'll be teaching you how to fly and I just wanted to see what I'll be working with.'

'I have to have flying lessons?' Becky asked. 'I thought I'd just be able to fly on my own.'

'Oh no, it's really tricky to learn how to fly, you have to be really patient, it can sometimes take weeks.' Said Tendril, 'but I'm afraid we don't have weeks for you to learn, so you'd best be a quick learner.' Becky didn't answer, she'd never learned anything quickly and she was pretty sure she wouldn't master flying too quickly either. 'Don't worry though.' Tendril said, putting her hand on Becky's shoulder, 'you'll be fine, luckily for you I'm the best flying teacher in The Kingdom.'

Just then Delphine and Esme walked back in with huge piles of food stacked in their arms, bits were dropping off with each step they were taking and Frankie swooped down and gobbled up what he could. The food all looked very weird and exotic to Becky, everything seemed to be bright colours and funny shapes, there was no meat at all, just lots and lots of fruit and veg, some of it cooked but most if fresh from the ground. Delphine and Stanton went to work cutting it up and dishing it out onto platters, in next to no time they had prepared a meal fit for a king, or a returning princess.

The Six Crew and their guests ate and drank and partied long into the night, Becky and Esme were the first to go to bed. They'd had a long journey and a lot of excitement and they were practically asleep on their feet when Tendril showed them where they'd be sleeping. They were to share the biggest bed, in the far corner, under the window. Both girls were asleep almost as soon as their heads hit the pillow, Becky was far too tired to even have bad dreams and they slept long into the next day.

CHAPTER 33

Becky was woken the next morning by the sound of laughter, not just any laughter, Delphine's laughter, Delphine's excited laughter, it seemed to go on and on. Becky lifted her head off the pillow and looked out the window, the Ergo Six Crew and Aunt Sylvia were all sat around the fire, eating and drinking, Becky was beginning to think that was all they did here. She looked round the cabin, sure enough, her and Esme were the only ones still in bed and it looked like the others had been awake for a while.

Becky tried to be quiet so as not to wake Esme but as soon as she moved to get out of bed Esme woke up. She was often grumpy in the morning and this morning was no different.

'What time is it?' Esme asked, wiping the sleep from her eyes.

'No idea' said Becky, 'but I think it's pretty late, I hope they're not mad at us.'

'Come on, Becs, let's go outside.'

They got up and stumbled outside, both of them had sore heads from the beer and bad backs from their bed.

'Here they are.' Said Colby, running over to them giving them both big hugs, 'Lazysaurus One and Lazysaurus Two. Did you both sleep okay?'

The girls smiled and nodded, both rolling their eyes at Colby. Tendril ran up behind Colby and hugged them both as well.

'How are you feeling, girls?' she asked with a huge grin on her face. 'Fresh enough to come training with me today, I hope? I've got a long day of training planned, first off is flying training, are you ready?'

Becky's head was whirling at a hundred miles an hour, she was already hungover and she didn't think trying to learn to fly would help her chances of recovery much, she looked over at Esme, who was looking a bit green. 'Could we have one more day to recover, Tendril?' Esme asked. 'I mean, we had a long journey yesterday and we've only just arrived, could we spend some time getting used to being in The Kingdom?'

'Hhhmmmm, okay then.' Said Tendril, 'you can have one more day to relax but you get an early night tonight, and not too much beer, do you hear me? We'll have a long day tomorrow so I don't want either of you looking like you look now.'

Both girls smiled 'thanks, Tendril,' said Esme, 'what should we do instead?' she asked.

'You can both come with me.' Said Ergo, he was busy pushing a trailer round the swamps. 'I've got to fill this trailer with the beer bottles and take them back to our supplier, it's not too far away but it will give you a chance to get to know the area a bit. I mean, granted it's not the nicest place in The Kingdom but The Swamplands still has some charm to it.' He stopped to look around and took a deep breath through his nose, 'I'm leaving in half an hour so you'd better get some breakfast and something to drink, I'll meet you back here.' He carried on pushing the trailer until he got to the steps of their hut then he went inside, banging his head on the lintel of the door and cursing again.

CHAPTER 34

Thirty minutes later, after the girls had eaten as much of the weird looking fruit for breakfast as they dared, Ergo stomped into camp and politely stood, waiting for them to join him. They both stood up together and walked over to where Ergo was, he smiled and turned around, walking behind their hut into a small clearing where a handsome horse was chewing the moss. The trailer had been attached to the horse, Ergo waved his arm towards the trailer, 'your carriage awaits, my ladies' he said, trying to sound as regal as he could.

'Thanks, Ergo' said Esme as they climbed into the uncomfortable looking trailer, they were both too grateful for the sit down to worry too much about comfort, their legs were still aching from all the walking yesterday.

'This is Anvil, my trusty horse and best friend.' Said Ergo, gently stroking Anvil's nose. 'He's going to pull you along and show you some of the sights of The Swamplands, there isn't too much to see other than swamps and trees but there's a few hidden treasures, so keep your eyes peeled.'

Off they went, Anvil leading the way, pulling the carriage over the bumpy, boggy terrain while Ergo walked alongside trying to think of something to say to the young ladies who were now in his care for the afternoon. The path wound around the swamps and every now and again led them through shallow swamps, Anvil was used to pulling the trailer through the swamps and they barely slowed down as they waded through.

Occasionally they'd hit a bump big enough to nearly throw them out of the carriage, Ergo was terrified they were going to fall out but the girls found it hilarious and Anvil, sensing their delight at the rocky journey, played up to it and started to speed up towards the bumps as Becky and Esme squealed in delight and laughed their socks off. Ergo was not impressed with this and kept scalding Anvil, who paid no attention, he was too busy showing off to his audience.

Once the excitement settled down, Ergo started chatting to the girls as he walked alongside the trailer, 'so' he said, 'how are you finding things so far?'

They looked at each other, each waiting for the other to answer, Becky started, 'a bit weird to be honest' she said, crinkling her nose slightly as she tried to think of an honest answer 'amazing, don't get me wrong, but weird as well.' She thought some more about how much things had changed for her in the last forty eight hours.

'I mean, the day before yesterday was a normal day of going to school and being bullied and having no friends apart from my family, and now.' She looked round at the trees, the swamps, the exotic monkeys in the trees and Frankie, her colourful new friend who had perched on her shoulder again. 'Now, I'm on a different planet with people who want me to go to war with them. Yes, definitely weird, Ergo.' She smiled at him, worried that he might take offense at her calling things weird.

'Ha' said Ergo in reply, 'well, I hope you're both prepared for things to get weirder, The Kingdom gets stranger the closer you get to Hightown Castle, often not in a good way.'

'What do you mean?' asked Esme.

'Well, there are creatures out there that are lethal, they're working for Gelda and they're looking for elves and fairies, just like us.' He paused for a while before breaking into a smile and trying to offer some comfort. 'But don't worry' he said, 'we've got some creatures of our own on our side and they're out to hurt Gelda and the trolls, so all should be fine.'

All three of them doubted anything would actually be fine, but none of them said anything. Just then, there was a break in the trees and right there in front of them, bathed in dark skies but lit up inside was Hightown Castle. This was a much better view than they'd had at the top of the mountain in The Wastelands, they were much closer now and could pick out small green dots moving around outside the castle, some walking, some riding big creatures. Although they couldn't make out exactly what the small dots were, they all knew they were trolls. As for the creatures some of them were riding on, Ergo was grateful he couldn't see them up close here, he'd seen one up close before and he'd never forget it.

'How can it possibly be so dark up there?' Asked Esme, 'the sun's out here, surely it should be out there as well.'

'It's dark magic, my friend.' Said Ergo, 'dark magic that's not to be messed with. Now come on, there's someone we need to meet and it will soon be dark here too.'

Anvil trotted along at Ergo's command, he had clearly been spooked by something and wasn't looking where he was going. He dragged the trailer straight into a murky green swamp, one wheel fell in and immediately started sinking. Before anyone knew what was happening, the trailer started tipping up and the bottles all clattered to the floor.

Becky Bigteeth

Ergo lurched forward and grabbed the side of the trailer, pulling it back down just before the two girls were sent flying. Anvil pulled with all his might to drag the trailer out of the swamp but he seemed to be getting himself even more stuck. Ergo ran around the trailer and stood next to Anvil, he put both his arms under the horse's body and heaved with all his might. Suddenly, he had the horse in his arms and was pulling him and the trailer away from the swamp and away from danger.

Once they were on the side, Ergo sat down, exhausted from his efforts. Becky and Esme hugged each other, they'd been terrified of falling in the swamp, it looked so murky and uninviting that they both feared if they fell in, they'd never get out again. Becky started crying hysterically.

'Hey, Becs, it's okay.' Said Esme as she hugged her cousin tightly. 'We're safe now, don't worry, it's okay.'

'NO! It's not okay!' Becky shouted, trying to free herself from Esme's grip, 'it's not okay at all, Esme, and we're not safe, of course we're not safe, look around, look where we are. There's danger everywhere, there are things out there want to kill us, Ergo said so himself, we're clearly not safe.'

Esme didn't know what to do, she hadn't been prepared for this outburst, she hadn't realised how scared Becky was. Ergo walked over and put his huge arms round them both while Anvil tried to stroke them both with his nose.

Just then there was a rustling in the bushes close to where they stood, they froze where they were and tried to work out where the noise was coming from. Anvil started flaring his nostrils and making snorting noises, Ergo shushed him gently and pulled his club from his belt, ready to strike whatever was in the bushes.

Dan Watford

The creature in the bushes walked out, Ergo ran forward with his club held high, ready to strike, just before he landed a blow on the creature, he stopped in his tracks. It wasn't a creature but a person, an elf more precisely, an elf that was too busy reading a map to notice the danger right in front of him. 'Nixon' said Ergo, quietly laughing, more from relief than actual humour, 'lower the drawbridge, Nixon, what are you doing out here making so much noise?'

CHAPTER 35

'Girls' said Ergo, smiling and walking towards the elf he'd called Nixon, 'this is a good friend of mine and of all the Six Crew and he'll be a good friend to both of you as well, this is Nixon.' He put his arm round him, 'Nixon, this is Becky and Esme, our newest recruits.'

'Boggle me, Ergo' said Nixon 'these are the latest recruits? I didn't realise things had gotten quite so bad, look how small their wings are, how scrawny they both look. Are we that desperate we're recruiting kids now?'

If Ergo was offended by this he didn't show it, he just smiled and asked Nixon if he had company.

'Don't worry, Ergo' said Nixon, 'we're all alone out here at the minute, there were some trolls around yesterday but they just wanted some beer before heading back to camp, there's not a troll within two miles of here.'

Ergo relaxed slightly 'Look closely at Becky, Nixon' he said, 'does she remind you of anyone?'

Nixon frowned at Ergo and looked a bit closer at Becky, then he looked at Esme, the girls were both uncomfortable at being studied so closely. 'They both look vaguely familiar to be honest but I can't put my finger on it. How long have you lived in The Swamplands for? You both look thin enough to have survived on the swamp diet for a couple of years, are you long termers?' He stared at them waiting for an answer, the girls were too confused to reply. 'Lower the drawbridge Ergo, can these two even talk? Are they original swamp stock?'

'Nixon' said Ergo, slowly losing patience, 'take your time and look at them closely, can you really not think who they look like?'

Nixon exhaled loudly, pushed his glasses further up his nose and took another step towards Becky and Esme. He stared at them from almost point blank range for about twenty seconds before he suddenly burst into a wild laughter, 'my goodness Ergo, you've done it haven't you?' he grabbed Ergo by the collar, smiling as widely as he could, 'you've actually done it, you've brought her back!'

Becky and Esme smiled at each other, relieved that they weren't being stared at anymore. They looked at Ergo, who was smiling as well. Suddenly Nixon dropped to his knees, 'forgive me Your Highness,' he said, bowing his head and holding his hands up, 'forgive me for my ignorance. My goodness, fancy keeping you out here on my doorstep, please come in, come in.' He ushered them inside, the girls went in first, followed by Ergo. Nixon slapped him round the back of the head as he walked past, 'Ergo, fancy letting me make such a fool of myself.' They both laughed and went inside.

CHAPTER 36

Nixon's place was a mess, it looked more like a brewery than a home. There were full beer bottles, empty beer bottles, barrels, and so many other contraptions for making beer strewn around the place, that they could barely move. Becky and Esme were both disappointed, Nixon was clearly more concerned with making beer than helping defeat Gelda. They wondered why they were wasting valuable time here.

'Sorry about the mess' Nixon said, 'I've had so many orders for beer since the trolls started camping nearby, it's kind of taken over my life. Well,' he said, looking at Ergo and smirking, 'it's taken over my normal life, but not my secret life.' He smiled even wider.

'Secret life?' asked Becky.

Nixon had been waiting for them to ask and wasted no time in answering, 'yes, you see, I have a public front which the trolls all know about, maybe even Gelda and Aldeese know about. But I also do some private work for the Six Crew.'

'That's right' said Ergo, putting his arm round Nixon. 'this is our secret weapon. Nixon can tell us exactly where all of the troll army are and exactly when and where they plan to move. We normally know what they're going to do next before they do, all thanks to Nixon.'

'Well, not quite.' Nixon said, frowning, 'the trolls used to tell me everything about Gelda's plans but just recently a lot of them havc kept things close to their chest. Some have given me tips and inside information, thinking I'm just a local brewer with no interest in the upcoming war. But a lot of them just ignore me now except to ask for beer.' He started to walk to the back of the cabin, 'come on, I'll show you my secret war room.'

Becky and Esme followed him through a small door at the back of the cabin, it looked like a little cupboard at first but they watched as Nixon pushed through some coats at the back and disappeared. They looked at each other quickly, neither one sure if they should follow before Esme shrugged her shoulders and pushed her way through, Becky followed right behind with Ergo just behind her.

The small cupboard led into a small, very warm room with a table in the middle and just enough room for them all to stand round the table. There were different coloured figures all over a map on the table and a castle right in the middle, small, scrawny handwriting was all over the map.

'You may have gathered,' said Nixon, 'that this is a small map of The Kingdom, this' he said pointing to the castle, 'is Hightown Caste, the most important building on Elfaron. And these lands further out are The Woodlands, The Swamplands, The Wastelands and The Wetlands.

'These small green figures represent us, the elves and fairies. The big green and blue figures represent the trolls, their numbers are growing all the time and no-one knows how so many are getting to The Kingdom. They're clearly coming from Troll Island but how so many are getting across with so few ships is beyond all of us.

'They're growing in number and spreading out from Hightown Castle, closer to us by the day. Their sole intention is to drive the elves and the fairies out of The Kingdom. We've already been driven out of the castle and out of the Woodlands, but as we speak Gelda, Aldeese and Velody are sending more trolls to force us out into The Wastelands.

'I have it on good authority that if we aren't out in the next two weeks, they're going to use force, Gelda is not known for her patience.'

'How long do you think we've got until they attack?' asked Ergo.

'Seven days.' Said Nixon, he didn't need time to think about it, 'it's Gelda birthday celebrations this week and she doesn't want the festival at the castle ruined so she's happy to wait until the day after her big party, but as soon as that's done I fully expect them to swoop down on us and start driving us out.'

Ergo said nothing, he just stared at Nixon for a long time, trying to digest what he'd just said and formulate a plan in his head. He couldn't do it, there just wasn't enough time to build a big enough army. He looked over at Becky and smiled, 'I think you've come home just in time, Becky. I hope you're good at leading people into battle because it looks like you'll be doing it sooner than expected. Thanks for the info, Nixon.' He said, shaking his hand as they got up to leave. 'Must go, we've obviously got lots to plan. When are you coming to join us?' he asked.

'Oh, a few days yet.' Said Nixon, 'I don't want to arouse suspicion amongst the trolls. And besides, you can do all the heavy lifting before I get there if I wait a while.' Nixon kissed both Becky's and Esme's hands and walked them to the door. 'Thanks for coming back to save us' he said as they left. Becky thought he was joking but when he didn't laugh, she realised he was deadly serious.

The journey home was sombre. Anvil could sense the tension and decided against any of his high jinks from the journey out, instead he kept his head down and rushed them back to camp as quick as he could. Ergo tried, and failed, to lighten the mood by making small talk about the weather but it did no good. Becky and Esme were too deep in thought to respond.

CHAPTER 37

It was dark by the time they made it back to the ranch, fortunately the mood in camp was far more upbeat which helped Esme and Becky forget about their problems, at least for a short while. Delphine was cooking over the fire and taking a sip from her tankard every couple of seconds, she was clearly celebrating being back home.

'Hhhheeeyyyy. You're back.' She shouted and staggered over to greet them. 'Everyone, hey everyone, they're back.'

'That's great, Delphine, thanks for pointing out the obvious for us.' Colby said as he got up to help them off the trailer. 'So' he asked, 'how was your day out with Ergo? He didn't bore you to death, did he?'

'Quite the opposite actually.' Said Becky, keen to spring to Ergo's defence. 'we had a great time, didn't we, Esme?'

'Oh yes. And we met Nixon.' Said Esme.

'Of course!' said Delphine, she was still practically shouting despite being stood right next to them, 'you went to see Nixon. How is the old bookworm?'

'He's fine, Delphine, everything's fine.' Ergo said as he unhooked the trailer from Anvil's saddle. 'We need to talk about things though, not out here, it's too dangerous. Everyone.' He said raising his voice so everyone in camp could hear him. 'Inside now, we've got a lot to discuss.'

'But I'm in the middle of cooking dinner.' Said Delphine, throwing her arms round at the fire to prove her point.

'It can wait Delphine, this is far more important than dinner.' Ergo turned to go in the cabin, everyone else followed, leaving Becky and Esme to help Delphine take the pot off the stove.

'More important than dinner.' Delphine said, under her breath, 'nothing's more important than dinner. Him of all people should know that.' Between them they lifted the pot off the fire and headed inside, they were the last ones in. Ergo was just about to start talking but waited for them to shut the door behind them. Frankie landed on Becky's shoulder and the three of them sat down near the door.

Martinez was stood next to Ergo and the pair of them were whispering to each other, this gave Becky another chance to study Martinez, she was fascinated by him. She was sure he was as nice as the others but there was something about him that seemed to set him apart and it wasn't just the obvious thing that his skin was much more blue than green. She wondered how many more blue elves there were in The Kingdom, she certainly hadn't seen another but she knew that didn't mean there weren't any more.

'Listen up, everybody.' Martinez said, loudly enough for everyone to hear, the murmuring died down straight away. 'As we know, Ergo has been to see Nixon, our eyes and ears in the field, and he wants to share his findings with us all.' With that, Martinez went back to join the audience, most of whom were now sat on the floor cross legged.

Ergo looked nervous as he started talking, Becky was amazed that someone so big and strong could be nervous about talking, it made her feel better about her own shyness. 'Thanks,

Martinez.' Ergo said before coughing to clear his throat. 'That's right, me, Becky and Esme have been to see Nixon today to see how much time we've got before the trolls start their next move. Which as we've all suspected for some time now is to drive us out into The Wastelands.'

'Nixon has confirmed that this is the plan. He hasn't been told outright by the trolls as they're a lot more secretive these days than they used to be, but he's heard them talking amongst themselves while buying beer from him. Things are worse than we feared, there are troll camps just five miles away from us here and they move slowly towards us every couple of days.'

'So how long have we got left before they get to us?' asked Colby, he was stood with Delphine next to a window so she could get some fresh air.

'I was just coming to that.' Said Ergo. 'Tonight marks the start of Gelda's birthday celebrations, seven days of feasts and fireworks. A lot of the trolls will be heading back to the castle to join the celebrations so they'll only leave a few hundred in the field but as soon as that's done, one week from today, they're planning to head back out and drive us away.'

'Seven days?' Delphine asked, this sobered her up quickly. The rest of the hut started murmuring amongst themselves, it wasn't quite panic but it was close.

'Quiet.' Said Martinez, immediately shushing the cabin. 'Let Ergo finish then we can all talk about what we're going to do. Ergo, what did Nixon suggest we should do?'

Ergo looked round a bit uneasy, 'well, he didn't really suggest anything, I thought it would be best to come back here and make plans. Stanton, what weapons have we got? How's our armoury looking?' Ergo was pleased to have diverted some of the attention away from him.

Stanton was a bit caught out by the question but slowly stood up and cleared his throat. 'Not too bad actually, Ergo. Our amptors are coming along well, we've currently got twenty-seven cannonspers and twenty-one herrows. I've been working on a few more things but nothing else is working out how I'd hoped, plus, our two blacksmiths have been working non-stop over the last few months to make sure we've got more than enough weapons and armour to go around.'

'Hang on' said Colby, still leaning against the window, 'so you're telling me that we plan to go into battle against Gelda, Aldeese and Velody, who currently hold Hightown Castle and are protected by who knows how many trolls, and have booby trapped The Woodlands all the way to the castle, not to mention them controlling the weather. And we plan to go into battle with them in seven days? And there's eighty of us and a few amptors? Are we all mental?'

Ergo and Stanton looked at each other, neither one sure what to say, the others looked away, everyone felt awkward. Frankie, sensing the unease in the hut, buried his face in Becky's neck.

Suddenly Martinez stood up, 'a lot can happen in seven days, Colby.' He said, 'we still have time to recruit more soldiers, Stanton and Nixon still have times to make more amptors for us, and now you're back with the Prophecy, we will have right on our side. The Gods will know we're destined to win this battle and they'll give us safe passage to the castle to defeat Gelda.'

Becky Bigteeth

'The Gods?!' shouted Delphine as she staggered slightly into the centre of the hut, 'the Gods? What have your precious Gods done for you recently, Martinez? If I remember rightly, you were talking about how the Gods would help us all before we left, that was fifteen years ago. What have they done for you while we've been away? They've allowed you all to be driven out of the castle, then out of The Woodlands and before too long they'll allow you to be driven out of The Swamplands. And you still want to preach about how the Gods are going to help us?'

Martinez looked wounded for a second, then regained his composure, 'Delphine' he said, 'the Gods knew it wasn't our time, they knew we had to wait for the true Prophecy to return. Just you wait and see, they know now is the right time. They'll make sure we win.'

Delphine exhaled and shook her head, turned around and walked out the cabin, Colby followed behind her, 'leave her, Colby' said Ergo, 'let her go and sober up, we still need to talk.'

Becky and Esme both thought about following Delphine outside to make sure she was okay but before they could make a move, Tendril came over.

'Right, you two, off to bed.' She said pointing to the beds in the corner, 'we've got a full day of training tomorrow and there's no getting out of it. You heard, we've got seven days. Seven days to turn you two into warriors. I want you both asleep in the next five minutes.' She walked off before either of them could argue, Becky admired Tendril's magnificent wings as she walked away. The girls went to the makeshift bathroom and went to bed, neither of them felt sleepy and they both had so many questions about tonight's meeting, they thought they'd be awake for hours, but as soon as they lay down, they both fell asleep.

CHAPTER 38

Becky overslept again and jumped out of bed when she noticed that Esme was already up. She wasn't sure if she was excited or nervous about the training but she knew she needed a wee. She found Esme outside, already sat on Anvil ready to go while Tendril flew around him, filling his carry bags with food, drink and weapons.

'Hurrah' said Tendril, 'you've both made it on time, well done, it looks like you cut it fine though, Becky. Come on, hop up on Anvil as well, the earlier we leave the less likely we are to bump into any trolls.'

Becky grunted and climbed onto Anvil, sitting behind Esme, as soon as she was on, Anvil started to trot off. Becky looked around for Frankie but she couldn't see him anywhere, probably still asleep, she thought.

It was more difficult for Anvil to get the girls wet today as they were sat on his back rather than in his trailer but still, he gave it a good go. Whenever he saw a puddle or swamp small enough to not fall in but big enough to make a big splash, he put his head down and ran towards it. The girls both thought it was hilarious and rather than tell him off like Ergo had done, Tendril encouraged him, laughing and clapping more with each splash.

Tendril kept flying ahead to scope out their route before flying back to have a quick chat with the cousins. She said she was keeping an eye out for trolls, they were normally okay, she said, but given what was happening at the minute, she didn't think it would be safe to be spotted. Especially seen as Becky looked so much like Gelda and they had carry bags full of weapons, it was deemed too dangerous to be seen.

Their training was to take place high up one of the mountains near the border of The Woodlands. It took them a couple of hours to reach, and the view was changing constantly. It had been almost dark when they set off even though it was late morning, now it was broad daylight and the sunshine warmed them all up nicely. The swamps started to thin out, giving way to a more mossy, firmer ground which made it easier for Anvil to power through and curtailed his splashing game.

Rather than just woods, The Woodlands actually appeared to be almost jungle, there were vines hanging down from the trees which reminded Becky of Tarzan and the animal noises they could hear were almost deafening at points. It sounded like a huge troop of monkeys were gathered in the trees next to them and were making as many loud screeching noises as they could. When the monkeys stopped, the birds started, all whistling a different tune, as loudly as possible.

They reached the bottom of the mountain without incident, Anvil was reluctant to start the climb so Tendril had to coax him with a carrot and the promise of an extra feedbag when they got home. He grunted, put his head down and started to climb up. Esme was fascinated with the wildlife and couldn't stop pointing out all the weird looking animals out to Becky. They could see fancy coloured birds that looked like parrots only bigger and brighter. Oddly, it seemed that Tendril could communicate with the birds, the girls watched fascinated as she whistled to them, nodded her head and even laughed with one of the birds.

Becky spotted some monkeys far away in the trees, they seemed very wary of the newcomers and stayed well back. The three of them watched as the biggest of the monkeys struggled to break open some fruit on the ground. 'Poor things' said Tendril, 'they normally break the fruit open with their teeth but the trolls have poached most of their teeth to make into jewellery to impress Gelda.'

'You're kidding.' Said Esme, 'that's awful.'

'It is.' Said Tendril, 'teeth have always been a status symbol in The Kingdom but ever since Gelda has been in power they've become even more important, the bigger your teeth, the more important you are. That's why you should never show your teeth to strangers, don't smile, don't eat anything, don't even breath through your mouth if you can help it. If word gets back to your mother that someone in The Kingdom has bigger teeth than her there's no telling what she'd do.'

Becky nodded and looked away, it was still hard for her to believe that she was powerful on this planet and the thought of her own mother wanting to cause her harm was too much for her to think about.

They carried on up the mountain in silence until Anvil grunted and stopped dead in his tracks, refusing to go any further. Tendril gave him a few more treats to snack on while they walked up the rest of the way on their own, each carrying a bag with their food and weapons in.

Tendril walked out from under the cover of the trees to have a drink from a stream, Becky and Esme followed her. As they looked upstream, they could see that right at the top of the mountain was a waterfall which flowed down into the stream they were drinking from and kept going down, eventually feeding all the swamps in Swampland.

'Come on.' Said Tendril once they'd all had a drink, 'we need to be at the top of the mountain, we'll do our training near the waterfall. Won't take long to get there.'